"I might drop in, depending on my parents' plans," Del said, and then, standing on the top step while he was two below her, she gave him a gentle kiss on the lips.

Nothing demanding, nothing deep and delving at first. Just a kiss between friends. That was the way she looked at it. Although the second kiss was more. It probed, and it was a real kiss—not just a friendly one. And it went on forever, grew in intensity until she was nearly breathless. Her face blushed and her hands trembled as she tried to bid him a nonchalant goodnight, which was nearly impossible to do given her rising feelings for him. So he didn't want a woman with a child. But she couldn't help the way she felt when she was around him, so what was she going to do?

"See you t-tomorrow," she stammered as her knees trembled on her way through the door.

But before she could get inside Simon gave her a long, hard kiss. This one was deep and abiding. The kind of kiss reserved for dates and special occasions. The kind that set her heart on fire.

Dear Reader,

Years ago a friend of mine decided to have a baby on her own. Her biological clock was winding down and her doctor said her baby-making days were limited. So she went through all the testing and finally had the baby she wanted—a fine, healthy baby girl. The joy of my friend's life. Back then it was scandalous, making that kind of decision. People talked about her, raised their eyebrows in speculation, but my friend withstood it all because she knew exactly what she was doing. And she never regretted a second of it, or the years since then. Today her daughter is on the verge of graduating at the top of her class from nursing school and she'll be an asset to her profession.

In my story Del finds herself in much the same spot. She wants the baby but doesn't want the man. Until she meets my hero she pictures herself in a life without a man, and she's quite happy there. Of course she meets the right man, and life changes for her. But in the meantime she proves that a woman *can* do it all and have it all these days. The old conventions no longer stand.

My friend never met the man of her dreams, but she was a strong, fantastic mother and one of the best nurses I'll ever know. All because that was what she chose for herself. So whether or not it's a traditional life doesn't matter. We can do it all if we have a mind to. My heroine does, and she finds just what she wants in her life. So did my friend.

Until next time, wishing you health and happiness,

DD

DOCTOR, MUMMY...WIFE?

BY

DIANNE DRAKE

Published in Great Britain 2016
By Mills & Boon, an imprint of HarperCollins*Publishers*
1 London Bridge Street, London, SE1 9GF

ISBN: 978-0-263-91500-6

nd recyclable
ests. The logging
onmental

Starting in non-fiction, **Dianne Drake** penned hundreds of articles and seven books under the name JJ Despain. In 2001 she began her romance-writing career with *The Doctor Dilemma*, published by Harlequin Duets. In 2005 Dianne's first Medical Romance, *Nurse in Recovery*, was published, and with more than 20 novels to her credit she has enjoyed writing for Mills & Boon ever since.

Books by Dianne Drake

Mills & Boon Medical Romance

Deep South Docs

A Home for the Hot-Shot Doc
A Doctor's Confession

Firefighter With A Frozen Heart
The Runaway Nurse
No.1 Dad in Texas
The Doctor's Lost-and-Found Heart
Revealing the Real Dr Robinson
P.S. You're a Daddy!
A Child to Heal Their Hearts
Tortured by Her Touch

Visit the Author Profile page
at millsandboon.co.uk for more titles.

Praise for
Dianne Drake

'A very emotional, heart-tugging story. A beautifully written book. This story brought tears to my eyes in several parts.'

—*Goodreads* on
P.S. You're a Daddy!

CHAPTER ONE

DR. DEL CARSON stumbled out of bed and groggily dragged herself into the nursery. A blue ceiling with white clouds, yellow walls with blue and white ducks and puppies greeted her as she turned on the overhead light and sighed.

"What now, sweetie?" she asked in a typically sleep-deprived thick voice as she trudged over to the crib and looked in at the six-month-old, who looked up at her and laughed at her with glee, as if he was eager to get his day started in the middle of the night. "Is it a diaper, or is this just your way of making sure your mommy doesn't get to sleep more than an hour at a time?"

Or maybe he just had her wrapped around his little finger; since it was just the two of them, she'd spent the first six months of his life catering to his every need.

It didn't matter, really. This was what she'd signed on for when she'd decided to become a mom, and any chance to make her baby's life better was welcome.

Tonight Charlie was particularly restless, all bright-eyed and ready to play, but, personally, she was played out. Even though the diaper seemed clean and dry, she changed it anyway out of habit, then sat down in the Victorian rocker, the one her mother had rocked her in, rocked little Charles Edward Carson until he was ready to go back to sleep for another hour. Two if Del was lucky.

Single motherhood was difficult, and she got all the support she could want from her family and friends. Being an only child, though, she missed the camaraderie of a sister or brother to take part in Charlie's life. He had no aunts or uncles, no cousins. Not on her side, and the father's side didn't matter since he was just a matchup on paper. A statistic that had struck her fancy.

It made her wonder sometimes if she should have another baby so Charlie wouldn't be raised in an isolated situation the way he was now. Del was a firm believer that children did better with siblings, and that was a thought she had tucked away in the back of her mind to visit in another year or two. "We'll get it worked out, Charlie," she said to the baby in her arms. "One way or another this will all have a happy ending."

The issue of single motherhood to deal with took an awful lot of hours when it was just the two of them—her and Charlie. She was continually amazed how much time someone so young could take up in the span of a single day. It was as if he'd hatched a plan to run away with every free second she had. But she loved it, loved her choice to become a mother on her own. No father involved, except Donor 3045, and she was grateful for his good genes because he'd given her such a healthy, beautiful child. The perfect child, as far as she was concerned.

She loved being a mother, even with the inconveniences. Loved spending time with her son. "My one and only true love," she would tell him. "For now it's just the two of us against the world."

Her parents lived in Costa Rica. They were supportive but not close by, which was one of the reasons she'd chosen to do this now. Her parents would have spoiled little Charlie rotten, and that was fine up to a point, but not to the extent she feared they might have gone. After all, five years in a horrible relationship had made them spoil her rotten when she'd finally found the courage to end it. That was just who they were, but she didn't want to raise a spoiled-rotten or privileged child. So they'd made their plans and, accordingly, she'd made hers. And she didn't regret it one little bit.

"Well, Charlie," she said as she put the baby back into his crib. "Are you going to let your momma sleep the rest of the night?" She was so tired she gave some thought to simply curling up in the rocker and pulling up a comforter. But little Charlie was fast asleep, so she held out some hope for three hours of sleep before he woke up and wanted to be fed, changed or just cuddled some more.

The life of a single mom. It wasn't easy, but she was taking advantage of it because in another two weeks' time she was trading in her maternity leave and returning to her medical practice with some on call and nighttime exclusions. Charlie was going to the hospital day care so she'd have easy access to him whenever she needed her baby fix. Sure, she was going to miss him. But she missed her old life, too, and she happened to be a staunch advocate of women who wanted it all. She certainly did. Every last speck of it except the part where there was a man included, and she wasn't ready to go there again. Not for a very long time to come. If ever again. And if she ever did that again he was going to have to be awfully special. Someone who'd love Charlie as much as she did.

Del, short for Delphine, sighed. She loved her work as a pediatrician in a private practice attached to Chicago Lakeside Hospital. In fact she had a passion for her work that couldn't be quelled by anything but work. Yet somehow, now that she was a mom, she knew her sensibilities had changed. To a doctor who now had a child, those little coughs and colds meant so much more. And when a mother's instinct dictated something wasn't right, the mother's instinct won. Being a mother-pediatrician rather than a plain old pediatrician was going to be a big advantage and, as much as she hated thinking about leaving Charlie behind for her work hours, she was looking forward to getting back to her normal life and trying to make all things fit together. It wasn't going to be easy, but if there was one thing Del was, it was determined, and she was determined to make sure all things worked together in her life.

"Good night again, love," she said quietly as she tiptoed from the room, turned on the night-light and lumbered down the hall back into her own bed. Unfortunately, sleep didn't happen as quickly as she'd hoped, and she lay awake staring off into the dark for about half an hour before her eyelids finally drooped. "I'm a lucky woman," she whispered into the dark as she was drifting. "I have everything." A beautiful child, a strong, supportive family, a good job. Best of all, no man to interfere.

She'd given away five *long* years to a man, always holding out the hope that he was the one who would complete her life. Problem was, he was completing the lives of several other women while she and Eric were going nowhere. So when she finally opened her eyes at the five-year point and took a good, hard look at the situation, she kicked him to the curb and decided she was in charge of creating and fulfilling her own dreams. No one else except one anonymous sperm donor needed.

It was a good choice, and as she drifted off to sleep, she did so with a smile on her lips.

Dr. Simon Michaels took a look out over the receptionist's shoulder at all the mothers and fathers waiting with sick children. It was cold and flu season, and if he didn't pick up the bug from one of these kids it would be a miracle. "How many more do I have to see?" he asked Rochelle, the girl at the desk. Rochelle was a tiny little thing who looked like one of the patients, and by comparison Simon felt he overshadowed her by a good foot. He, with his broad shoulders and longish brown hair, had to make sure he didn't treat Rochelle as a kid because, after all, she was well over twenty-one, and very efficient in her job.

She looked over the top of her glasses then laughed. "That's just what's left of the morning appointment block. You're going to have at least that many this afternoon, and tonight's your night for on call, so look out. Around here we look at Halloween as scary but not for the same reason most people do. We'd much rather see a goblin than a flu bug."

"Any word on when the mysterious Del Carson will be back?" He'd been hired to replace Del during her leave, then asked to stay on as a permanent member of the pediatrics clinic team. He'd heard of Del, but never met her. In fact, what he'd been told was that she was an excellent doctor, if not an overprotective mother who didn't want to come in for fear that she might contract some disease and take it home to her baby. He didn't know if that was true or not, but the only truth he knew was that she was merely a name in passing. Someone who would be his boss when she returned.

"Be patient," Rochelle warned. "She'll get here when she's ready. That new baby of hers is taking up a fierce amount of her time right now, but I expect she'll be back in a couple weeks or so, if she doesn't change her mind and stay home another half year." Rochelle smiled. "She loves being a mother."

"And there's no father?"

Rochelle shook her head. "Her choice. And she's proud of it, not shy in the least to talk about it."

"Well, that's something you've got to admire—a woman who knows what she wants and goes out and gets it." It couldn't be easy, and it would get a whole lot more difficult once she was back at work. He wondered if she fully realized what she was letting herself in for. "Can't wait to meet her. It will be nice having more help," he said, even though it wasn't his intention to complain. And he wouldn't. After all, he had a job in the location of his dreams. He was finally back home in Chicago after all those years in Boston and, as they said, "There's no place like home."

In fact, he lived only a few blocks from where he was raised. All within sight of the Navy Pier and the lakeshore. It was good. Pediatrics was such a full field here, though, that when he'd got the call to come and interview, he couldn't believe his good luck. No place at County Hospital, no place at Lakeside. Just no place. Then this spot came open—the pediatric clinic attached to Lakeside—and it was a godsend at a time that couldn't have suited him any better. Divorced from Yvette, who hadn't turned out to be the woman he'd thought she was, working in a practice where he was clearly never going to advance, cynical about life in general, feeling as if the whole world were closing in around his bad choices… Coming home was better, even if his workload was crazy big right now.

What the hell did that matter, though? It wasn't as if he had anything else going on in his life other than his work—a situation that suited him just fine. In fact, to avoid some of the long lonely nights he even took call for his colleagues just to give him something to do. Some might call it crazy, but he called it picking up the pieces of his broken life.

"So the plan is for her to be back in two weeks?" He grimaced. There were two weeks of work waiting to see him right now, and he was the only general pediatrician in the house today. The other two had succumbed to the virus that was being spread like wildfire. Leaving him to roll up his sleeves and just pitch in, keeping his fingers crossed that he stayed healthy so he could handle the workload.

Pulling up his surgical mask and snapping on a fresh pair of gloves, he sighed. “Send in the next one.”

Rochelle chuckled. “Wouldn’t it just be quicker to go out there, sit them in a circle and look at them as a group?”

“What would be easier would be flu shots. But people don’t think about getting vaccinated until they’re already sick with the flu.”

She pointed to her upper arm. “Got mine. Hope you got yours.”

“I’ve been a pediatrician too long not to.” But that didn’t mean he wasn’t susceptible. Because vaccinations weren’t foolproof, as his colleagues had discovered.

Two more weeks and Del Carson might reappear. Admittedly, after six months of hearing glowing reports about her, he was anxious to meet her. “You don’t suppose we could convince Dr. Carson to come back early, do you?” he asked as he grabbed up the next patient chart. Five years old, fever, runny nose, cough, generally out of sorts.

“She values her baby time. She’ll be back when she’s back.”

Of all the bad timing to be on leave... He signaled for his nurse, Ellie Blanchard, and off they went, back to work. Vaccinating children and parents alike, dispensing antinausea medicine, and generally just trying to make it through the day. “Next,” he said as he stepped into Exam Four. “And get me two more ready to go. We’ve got a lot of patients to see in the next hour.”

Glancing up at the clock on the wall, he shook his head. Not enough time. Not nearly enough time even if he worked through his lunch hour.

No trying to hide it, she had tears streaming down her cheeks as she handed Charlie to the day-care director then headed down the winding walkway to the clinic. It wasn't as if she didn't trust the center to take good care of him. They had an excellent reputation and the staff in general spoke very highly of them—but this was her baby she was handing over and being only a building away didn't make any difference. She hated doing it. Considered at the very last minute whether or not she was ready to go back to work or if another six months' maternity leave might be called for.

But one look at the swamped clinic told her she was doing the right thing. Other children needed her, too. And admittedly, she did feel that tingle of excitement the moment she stepped through the front door—a tingle that told her she was back where she belonged.

There were lots of single moms just like her who left their children and went to work every day. She didn't have someone to support the two of them. It was up to her. Besides, she loved her work. Still, she was sniffling as she approached her office door and went inside. Leaving Charlie behind made her feel so empty, so alone. "Suck it up," she told herself as she pulled on her lab coat, the one with her name embroidered onto the pocket. "You knew this was how it was going to be when you did this."

Still, she hadn't counted on it being so difficult. "But

you're lucky," she said as she looked in the bathroom mirror and touched up her streaky eyes. "You've got excellent day care and you're only a few steps away." A few steps that seemed like miles. Damn it! She wanted to be home with her baby even though she knew she was needed here. Torn in half—that was how she felt. Completely ripped down the center.

Taking in a deep breath, she exited her office and stepped almost directly into the path of a doctor she didn't recognize. The new hire? "Sorry," she said, trying to find a smile for him even though it simply wasn't in her to be found.

"You must be Dr. Carson," he said, extending his hand to her.

She gripped it weakly. "And you are… Was that Dr. Michaels?"

"Call me Simon."

"And I'm Del," she said, appraising the hunk of man standing right in front of her. OK, so she'd vowed off involvement, but she could still look, and what caught her attention first, outside his very soft hands, were his stunning green eyes. They were serious, but she could almost picture them smiling and sexy.

"Well, Del, I'm glad you're finally back. We've been too busy to make much sense of our patient load for a while, and we've needed you."

"My baby needed me more than the clinic did."

"I imagine he did," Simon said, "but you haven't been here and the pace has been crazy."

She looked over his shoulder to a normal waiting room. "Looks like things are under control to me."

"Want to know how long it's been since I've been able to take a lunch break?"

She laughed. "No guesses from me. We all have to make sacrifices, Dr. Michaels. Some bigger than others."

"You're referring to leaving your baby in day care?"

"That, and other things." But mostly that.

"Well, at least it's a good day care and nearby. That's an advantage for you."

"But I don't have to like it."

"All I said was I'm glad you're finally back. You were needed."

"And I appreciate that, but I was also needed at home." Where she wished she could have stayed. "But it's nice to be missed. I take it you don't have any children?"

He paused for a moment, then winced. "No children. Divorced. No future plans for anything except working."

"And yet you complain about too much work."

"Not complain so much as remark. We're busy here. We needed you. Simple as that." He chuckled. "Almost as much as you need me."

"Well, you've got me there. We do need you, especially right now."

Simon nodded. "During the flu outbreak the average wait time was an hour per patient. Which is too long for a sick kid to have to sit there and wait."

"See, you could have told me that right off."

"Pent-up frustrations," he said. "I've been working hard."

"I can see that." She smiled at him. "Well, you're

right. An hour is too long. We like to guarantee no more than twenty minutes. Shorter if we can get away with it."

"Sorry about my attitude, but all I could picture in my mind was you sitting at home playing with your baby when we had patients lined up in the hallways."

"Trust me, it wasn't all play. Babies require a lot of work."

"I know, I know. I'm think I'm just tired...I know it must have been hard work, especially on your own," he said.

"So how about we get off to a fresh start? Hello, I'm Del Carson and you're..."

"Simon Michaels." He held out his hand to shake hers and they both smiled. "So how was your maternity leave?"

"Great. I hated for it to be over with but all good things must end. So, how many patients do we have to see this morning?"

"About twenty, barring emergencies."

She nodded. "I'll grab some charts and get started."

"And after I get my foot out of my mouth, I'll do the same."

Del laughed. "You were right up to a point. I was entitled to my maternity leave and I don't regret taking it. But things shouldn't have gotten so out of control here at the clinic. Someone should have called me and I might have been able to get a couple of our specialists out here to help with the overflow."

"I tried," Simon confessed, "but I'll admit my attitude might have been better."

"I didn't read anything about a bad attitude in your

application or your letters of recommendation. And even though I never met you until just a few minutes ago, I called your superiors in Boston and they gave you glowing reviews."

"Probably anxious to get me out of there. I'm a pretty fair doctor but I do let things get to me too easily, I suppose. You know, take it all too personally."

"We all do at times. And I suppose especially the newcomer who's being the logical target." For a moment, a softness flashed through his eyes.

"Six months *is* a long time to be away."

"Not long enough," she replied. "I was actually thinking about another six, but I love my work as much as you seem to love yours. So I came back."

"Straight into the arms of a disgruntled employee."

"Nice, sturdy arms, though. And I'm willing to bet they hold no grudges."

"Me? Hold a grudge?" He laughed outright. "Grudge is my middle name. Ask my ex-wife."

"Think I'll stay out of the family problems."

"So, I understand you're raising your baby all on your own."

"Yes, it's just Charlie and me but that's the way I planned it."

"Well, I suppose that's the way to do it if you want to keep your autonomy."

"More like my sanity." They meandered down the hall to the clinic's nursing hub and she picked up the first chart off the stack. "And contrary to popular belief, I *am* sane."

"Reasonable, too, dealing with me as diplomatically

as you have this morning. I must confess that when I heard you were coming back I put together some mighty well-chosen words for you."

"So I noticed," she said as she opened the chart and looked at the info contained inside. "But they could have been worse." The first patient was a child named Sam with some sort of rash. Her first fear was a communicable rash and her next fear was that she might transfer something to Charlie. Truth was, if she didn't get over her irrational fears, she wasn't going to be any good as a pediatrician anymore. Most kids that came in were communicable and if she worried about carrying something home to her baby every time she came into contact with a sick kid, she'd drive herself crazy. Plus there was also the possibility that she might be too cautious to make a proper diagnosis. Obsession. That was what it was called. She had an obsession, and she wondered for a moment if she should seek professional help for it. But the instant she stepped in Sam's exam room and saw the rash she knew the poor kid was miserable. He was obviously allergic to something with which he was coming into contact.

"Does it hurt or itch?" she asked him.

"He scratches it like crazy," Sam's mother answered as Sam's eyes filled with big, fat tears.

"When did it start?"

"Three days ago?"

"What happened three days ago that changed his routine?"

"Nothing except...we went picking pumpkins in

the pumpkin patch for Halloween. He's not allergic to pumpkins, is he?"

"You've had pumpkins in your house before?"

"Every year," the mother replied.

"And what about the pumpkin patch?"

"This was our first year to go."

"I'm betting the rash is connected to the pumpkin plant."

"He's allergic to the plant?"

"Has there been anything else new introduced in his life since the rash popped up?"

"Not that I can think of," the mother answered, a frown on her face indicating she was thinking. "No new food, no new clothes, my laundry detergent hasn't changed."

"Then for now, let's go on the assumption that he has an allergy to the actual pumpkin plant and if the rash doesn't clear up in a few days or it comes back we'll investigate other possibilities and take some tests. For now, I'd rather save him the trouble, though. So, any of the over-the-counter hydrocortisone creams will help with the rash, and I'm going to give him a shot today that should speed things along."

She looked down at Sam, who looked back at her with big, sad eyes. "Will it hurt?" he asked.

"A little bit, but you're a big boy and you can take it." In reality Sam was only five and at an age where needles really scared kids. Some people never outgrew the phobia and she didn't want to make this too traumatic on this poor child. "Anyway, let me go get you some ointment samples, and have the shot prepared, and I'll be back in a couple of minutes."

True to her word, Del appeared back in Sam's room a few minutes later with a syringe full of antihistamine and a bag full of samples. Once she'd convinced Sam the needle wouldn't hurt that much, she gave him the injection, and wrote down instructions for his mother to follow, including the antihistamine to be taken three times a day in small doses. "This should clear up in about three days," she told Sam's mother on the way out. "If it doesn't, call me. In fact, call me either way because I'm curious if he is allergic to pumpkin vines. That's kind of an odd allergy..."

Actually, nothing in the allergy world was odd. People had reactions to everything—to the expected as well as the unexpected, as in Sam's case.

Her first day back dragged. She couldn't get herself into the rhythm to save her soul. And between her hourly calls to check on Charlie and her work she was ready to go home by noon. But she'd just have to understand that this was the way it was. She loved her baby and she worried. Although, by the time her fourth call rolled around, she was sure the child center over at Lakeside was probably sick of her calling. So she vowed to not call after she took her lunch hour with Charlie. Which turned out to be around one o'clock.

"Momma missed you," she said, picking him up and kissing him, then walking around the room with him.

"Am I being a nuisance?" she asked Mrs. Rogers, the director.

"Pretty much, yes," she answered, smiling. "But the first few weeks aren't easy. So we're pretty forgiving."

"I miss him, and it's all I can do to keep from coming over here, getting him and taking him home."

"You're not the first, and you won't be the last," Mrs. Rogers replied. She was an older woman, short gray hair, and a registered nurse, retired.

No one could have better credentials or more experience with children, and Del considered herself lucky that they'd had an opening for Charlie, as the child center was usually booked months in advance. As it turned out, she'd reserved a spot even before he was born in the anticipation of returning to work and the timeline had worked out perfectly.

Del sighed heavily as Charlie snuggled into her and dozed off. "It's amazing the way they can change a life so drastically, isn't it?"

Mrs. Rogers laughed. "Too bad we can't keep them all young and innocent, the way he is now. But if we did we wouldn't get grandbabies, and I've got to tell you there's a certain sense of satisfaction in being a grandmother."

"How many grandkids do you have?" Del asked her as she laid Charlie back down in the crib.

"Five, so far. One on the way."

"That's awesome," Del replied.

"What about your parents?"

"Grandparents in absentia. They live in Costa Rica and travel back every couple of months to spoil Charlie."

"No husband?"

Del shook her head. "By design it's just the two of us."

"I admire a woman who knows what she wants and goes out and gets it."

"And I admire you for taking such good care of all these children."

"My assistants and I love children, and, since we're all retired pediatric nurses, it's a good way to still stay involved."

Del smiled as she kissed her sleeping Prince Charming goodbye and returned to her clinic, feeling much more relieved than she had only an hour ago. In fact, this was the first time she thought it might actually work out, working full-time instead of part-time as well as being a full-time mom. At least, there was room for optimism in the scenario now. For which she was glad because she loved her work with a passion.

"Little Tommy Whitsett is here," Rochelle said to Simon as he left an exam room where the child had a blueberry stuck up his nose. "I think it's another case of nursemaid's elbow." Where a quick tug of a toddler's arm oftentimes resulted in partial dislocation of an elbow ligament. In Tommy's case it was a chronic condition, one caused when his older brother tugged a little too hard on Tommy's arm, causing the ligament to snap out like a rubber band and not reset properly. It was typical of toddlers and Tommy would most likely outgrow the tendency in another year or two, but until then there was nothing really fixable as it wasn't a serious injury. And the fix was easy. One gentle pop usually set the ligament right back where it belonged. Tommy got his lollipop and went home to have other wrestling matches with his brother.

"Have him shown to Room Three," Simon said, and joined Tommy there a moment later. This was the third time he'd seen the child for the same injury in the past couple of months.

"I'm sorry this keeps happening, Doctor," his poor, red-faced mother said. "But when they get to playing..." She shrugged.

"No big deal. He'll outgrow this eventually, and that will be that."

"But I feel so foolish coming in here so often. I'm afraid it might look to some like I'm an abusive parent."

Admittedly, at one time Simon had wondered if Tommy's handling at home was too rough, but he had a different attitude now that he'd met the cause face-to-face—a much bigger, sturdier brother—and witnessed the worry in Tommy's mother's face. "Boys will be boys. You just happen to have one who's a little more elastic than the other one ever was. No big deal. Maybe have a word with his big brother to try and persuade him pulling his brother's arm isn't such a great idea."

"I have tried, Doctor. It always scares me."

"A lot of mothers get petrified if their child coughs or sneezes. That's the proof of parenthood, I guess."

"You're not a parent, are you, Doctor?" she asked him.

He hesitated for a minute, then shook his head. "Haven't had that opportunity yet." If ever again.

"Well, it's not easy."

He thought back to Del and recalled the strain on her face at simply leaving her baby behind in a safe environment. Maybe he should have more empathy for her, going through separation anxiety as she was. But he found that difficult as he didn't know how to show it for someone who'd made deliberate choices. Like Yvette, who'd pulled Amy out of his life altogether. He'd been the only father the child had known, albeit he was the stepfather. Then when his ex-wife met someone else, his feelings for Amy didn't matter. So he was understandably still bitter and some of his personal reactions still reflected that. "You're right. It's not easy," he said to Tommy's mother.

"I guess," Tommy's mother said. "But I wish it was sometimes."

"Parenting is never easy. It makes us realize just how powerless we are in so many situations. And I know you hate that vulnerability, but in your case you've got two fine, healthy sons and at the end of the day that's quite an accomplishment."

"Let me tell you a secret, Doctor. There's never an end to the day. Parenting is so hard, and it never stops."

"And you love it, don't you?"

"Except for when I have to bring Tommy in for another case of nursemaid's elbow." She smiled. "But I wouldn't change a thing."

"Challenging case, Dr. Carson?" Simon asked after he walked Tommy and his mother back to the waiting room.

"If I thought you were interested because you were

really interested, I might answer that question, but somehow I think you'll snipe at me for taking the easy cases today since you're so distracted, so all I'll tell you is that we divide them as they come in and leave it at that."

"That's right. I'm not a partner. Just a lowly employee. I'm not privy to the inner workings of what goes on around here."

"You're causing a scene over a case of pinkeye?"

"You're treating pinkeye, I'm treating a kid with possible asthma. Are you going to tell me it all evens out?"

"I'm sorry for your diagnosis," she said sympathetically. "And if you'd rather not..."

"It's not that I'd rather not. But what I was wondering is if we get to pick and choose our cases or if we just get them according to what's up next, and who our established patients are."

"If you're trying to insult me, I have thick skin, Doctor."

"Not trying to insult you, Doctor. Just trying to figure things out now that you're back."

"Well, figure this out. It's a fair system. I don't take all the easy cases and assign the tougher cases to my colleagues. You were treating an easy case of nursemaid's elbow when I was treating a little girl with Erb's palsy. Unless a patient requests a specific doctor we take whoever's up next, regardless of the easiness or severity of their condition." She bit her tongue to hold the rest in but didn't do a very good job of it because the rest slipped out. She knew this had to be tough on

Simon, working in basically a new situation, especially with his credentials. "Trust me—it's fair."

"It's always good to know my standing."

"Sure it is. You got stuck in a jammed-up clinic when I was gone and you're blaming me for it. So now you want some answers. Can't say that I blame you. Reverse the situation and I'd be asking the same questions."

Simon kicked off his shoes and set his mug of coffee next to the sofa. Sighing, he popped an old classic movie into his DVD player then dropped down on the couch with his bowl of cold cereal, contented to spend the evening vegetating.

He'd gotten off to a rough start with Del and, to be honest, was surprised she hadn't fired him on the spot. There really was no excuse for his questions, especially when he knew the answers. But he'd been in the mood to antagonize someone and Del had seemed to be it.

The thing was, he'd called to talk to Amy this morning and was told by her latest stepfather that he had no rights to the girl any longer, to please not call back or he'd be served with a restraining order. Damn! He missed her. Red hair and freckles, with a little gap between her front teeth—sometimes he swore he'd stayed married to her mother just because Amy was so endearing. But that was obviously over and now he wasn't even allowed to talk to her any more. It hurt. It stung to the bone because he missed Amy with all his heart. Didn't know how he was going to get along without her. And Del, well...she'd just caught some of his fallout. Wrong place, wrong time and with a child who was making her so happy—happy the way he'd used to be.

Well, one thing was for sure. He'd never, ever get involved with a woman who already had a child. It just opened him up to getting hurt again.

In the meantime, he owed Del a big apology for being so confrontational over everything today. She didn't deserve it just because she'd had a child.

He owed her an apology and it wouldn't keep until tomorrow. He opened his clinic information packet and found her cell-phone number. On impulse, he dialed.

"Hello," she answered, almost in a whisper.

"Del, this is Simon Michaels."

"And?"

"I may have been a little harsh with you today."

"Not so I noticed," she lied. "It was a tough day for everybody."

"Still, I wasn't myself and I'm calling to apologize."

"No need. I wasn't at my best, either, this being my first day back and all. Look, you woke up my baby. I've got to go. Can I call you back?"

"No need for that. I just wanted to apologize."

"Thanks, Simon," she said, and with that she hung up on him. And he actually chuckled. She was interesting, to say the least. Definitely her own woman marching to her own beat.

CHAPTER TWO

"HE'S NOT VERY pleasant at times," Del said to Charlie as she gave him his nightly bath. "On the verge of rude and insulting. Then he calls and apologizes. Like what's that all about?" Although he did exude a general sexiness about him, which was nothing she was going to admit out loud. Even when brooding he was sexy and she wondered, for a moment, what kind of social life he had going for himself. "It's none of my business," she told Charlie. "And I want you to point that out to me every time I have a straying thought about the man. OK? He's handsome and has the ability to be charming, but that's as much as I want to notice."

The baby's response was to splash around in the water and giggle.

"I'm not sure why my partners would have chosen him, except for the fact that he's a good doctor, but that was their decision, not mine. And his credentials are good. At least he's licensed here in Chicago, which saved a little bit of hassle. But that attitude…I've got to tell you, Charlie, you're not going to grow up to be a man like he is, who goes back and forth. I'll swear by all that I know as a doctor and what I'm learning as a mother that you're going to have manners and respect." Yeah, until he was an adult; then he could do anything he wanted, which scared her because somewhere there was probably a mother who'd said the same thing to her baby Simon. And look at the way he'd turned out. "I suppose a mother can only do so much," she said as she pulled Charlie out of the baby bath and wrapped him in a towel. "But I'm going to teach you anyway and keep my fingers crossed I don't go wrong somewhere." Not to imply that Simon's mother had gone wrong. Because Simon did have manners and just a touch of arrogance to offset them.

"Now, let's get you dressed and I'll read you a story. How about the one with the giraffe, tonight?" Sure, it was all in her mind but she thought that was Charlie's favorite story. Of course, any story might have been his favorite, as he seemed delighted by everything she read him, including pages from a medical journal she'd read aloud to him one evening when she was trying to catch up on her own reading. It was the mother-child bond that mattered, the one she'd missed all day today while she'd been at work.

But on the other hand, work had had its number of fulfilling moments, too, and it was good getting back. She was still plagued with guilty feelings, though. Those weren't going to go away, and she could foresee the time when the conflicts would become even greater, such as when Charlie learned to walk, or started talking. She didn't want to miss those things, but it was conceivable he might say his first word to Mrs. Rogers or take his first step when she wasn't around to see it. Sacrifices. Yes, there were definite sacrifices to be made, and she could feel them tugging at her heart. But she was still drawn to being a pediatrician, and while she felt guilty about working she felt no guilt at all about the work she did. It would have been nice, though, to have that proverbial cake and eat it, too.

Well, that wasn't going to happen. She had a child to support now and her savings, while sufficient, weren't enough to carry her through until he went to college. So off to work, get over the guilt. She supposed in time it would lessen, but her preference would always be to be there for her son.

"Once upon a time, there was a giraffe named George, who was shorter than all the other giraffes in the jungle. 'Why can't I be tall like my mother?' he asked." This is where Del tickled Charlie's tummy with a stuffed giraffe. "'Why can't I be tall like my daddy?'" She tickled Charlie's tummy again and took such delight in watching him laugh and reach out to hold his giraffe. "'Why can't I be tall like my brother...?'" And so the story went, until Charlie usually wore himself out and went to sleep. Which was the case tonight. He dozed off before the end of the story, clinging to his stuffed giraffe, and she tucked him into his crib, crept out and made sure the night-light was on for when he woke up later as she hated the idea of her child waking up in total darkness and being afraid.

Afterward, Del fixed herself a cup of hot tea and settled down on the couch to catch up on some reading, but she was distracted by her cellphone, which she'd set to vibrate now that Charlie was down. She'd been awfully rude to Simon and for no reason other than Charlie couldn't wait a minute or two—which he could have since he hadn't been crying for her. She'd set a bad example for Charlie even if he was too young to understand that. But there would come a time when he would and she dreaded that day. So in the end, she picked up her phone and made that call.

"Simon," she said when he answered. "This is Del."

"Let me guess. You want me to go in tonight."

"You caught me at a bad time earlier," she said.

"Apparently."

"Look, I had just got my baby to calm down and go to sleep after his first day away from me, and you disturbed him. You're not a parent, so you wouldn't understand," she said.

"No, I'm not a parent," he answered, then sighed so loud into the phone she heard it.

"Well, you couldn't understand what I'm talking about, but I like my evenings undisturbed."

"Which is why you've begged off call for the next six months."

"It was a compromise. Originally I was going to take off a whole year to stay home with Charlie, but that didn't work out so I decided to come back during the days so long as I have my evenings and nights to myself."

"Not that it's any of my business."

"Look, Simon. I called to apologize for being so rude. We got off to a bad start and when you called to apologize I wasn't in the frame of mind to deal with it."

"Guilty-mother syndrome?"

"Something like that."

"I understand children, Del, but I don't even pretend to understand their parents."

"You would if you were a parent."

"Well, thank God I'm not. My marriage was hell and it makes me queasy thinking we could have easily brought a child into it."

"So you're divorced."

"Blessedly so."

"Sorry it didn't work out. Is that why you hate women?"

"Who says I hate women?"

"Your scowl, every time I looked at you today."

"Well, I don't hate women. I'm just…wary."

"Sorry you feel that way. Anyway, I just wanted to let you know I'm sorry I was abrupt with you on the phone earlier. Normally I silence my phone so I won't be disturbed, and people who know me know when to call and when not to call."

"I didn't get the memo," he said.

"Then I'll make it simple. Evenings are my time unless it's an emergency. That's the memo." He was impossible and she was already dreading working with him. But what was done was done. He was hired, the partners were happy with him and he was a hard worker. Everyone in the office shouted his praises, so it had to be her. He rubbed her the wrong way, or the other way around. Anyway, her feelings for the man were no reason to give him grief, so before she hung up the phone she made a silent vow to tolerate him in the office. If he did his job and she did hers there'd hardly be any time to socialize anyway.

"So, as I was saying, I'm sorry for being so abrupt and it won't happen again."

"Let's call it a professional standoff and leave it at that."

"Professional, yes, of course. But that's all. And just so you'll know, you don't even have to acknowledge me in passing if you don't want to."

"Wouldn't that look unfriendly?" he asked.

"Maybe. But who's going to notice."

"Everybody." He laughed. "Are you afraid of me?"

"No, not really. I'm just not in the mood to have a man in my life—especially one I'll be working closely with."

"You formed that opinion of me after one day?"

"I form fast opinions."

"You must. But just so you know, I don't hate you and I don't even dislike you. I got off to a bad start this morning because of some personal matters and it carried over. But it has nothing to do with you." He smiled gently. "In fact, I've felt bad all day for the way we got started."

"You did?" she asked.

"I'm not usually quite so abrupt."

"Neither am I."

They both laughed.

"So tomorrow maybe we get off on a better foot?" she asked.

"Well, now that that's settled, let me be the one to hang up this time." With that he clicked off.

* * *

Her second and third days at work went a little better than her first, but she still missed Charlie so badly. Her situation with Simon didn't improve, though. She tried being friendlier, and he reciprocated, not in an out-and-out way but at least in a friendlier manner. Still, to Del their relationship felt distanced. Cordial but not particularly friendly. And somehow she had the impression it didn't have anything to do with her. At least she hoped it didn't because she wanted them to be just a touch more than cordial.

It was the fifth day when he actually greeted her with some hospitality. "Would you mind taking over a case for me?"

"Symptoms?"

"First, he's four years and his mother admitted to some pretty heavy drinking during pregnancy."

"So let me list some symptoms for you. Poor impulse control, poor personal boundaries, poor anger management, stubbornness, intrusive behavior, too friendly with strangers, poor daily living skills, developmental delays—attention deficit/hyperactivity disorder, confusion under pressure, poor abstract skills, difficulty distinguishing between fantasy and reality, slower cognitive processing. Stop me when I hit five of these."

"You hit five of the symptoms a long time ago."

"So you know what it is?"

He nodded. "But you're the expert in treatment for FAS."

"I'll be glad to take a look and get started with a plan,

but you do realize that most treatments respond best to behavioral therapy. Poor thing's going to be saddled with a disability for his entire life."

"Well, you're the best one for the job," he admitted.

That took her by surprise. "Thank you. I appreciate the compliment," she said, almost stumbling over her words.

"Look, is there any chance we could start over… again?"

"Maybe," she said, hiding a smile. She liked this side of him and she was glad she was finally going to coax it out of him, if for no other reason than a better working relationship. "Is the mother or father more responsive now?"

"Child's under protective service. He has a foster family who really cares."

"That's a step in the right direction."

"Anyway, I told them we have an expert on staff so I'm leaving it up to you to schedule them in. I slid the note with his file reference under your office door."

"I appreciate the vote of confidence," she said.

"When you've got the best on staff you'd be crazy not to."

She didn't know whether to take that as a compliment or a disparaging remark in disguise. For a moment or two she'd been flattered, but now…she didn't know. It seemed more like a professional request and not something that spoke to his opinion of her abilities. Oh, well, she decided. It was what it was, whatever that might be. "I'll read the file and call the foster parents to see what we'll be addressing."

"I appreciate it," he said as he walked away.

"Do you really?" she whispered. "I wonder."

It was hard getting a beat on the good Dr. Del. One minute she seemed friendly enough and the next she was glacial. So, what was her game? Simon wondered as he watched her stride through the hall without so much as a glance in his direction. Did she hate men? Or did she feel that he jeopardized her position at the clinic? Whatever the case, they were barely any further along than they'd been two weeks ago when she'd first come back to work, and now it was becoming frustrating. While he didn't expect a friendship out of the deal, he did expect a civil work environment, which she barely gave him but only because it was required. And, it was getting to him. Maybe it was the whole social conquest of the deal but he did have to admit the more she stayed away, the more he wanted to get close. With her long, nearly black hair and her dark brown eyes, she had a drop-dead-gorgeous body that begged to be looked at and he enjoyed the looking.

Was she becoming a habit or an obsession? Maybe a little of both. But he wasn't the only man doing the looking. He was, though, the only one she treated with woeful disregard. Except in the professional capacity and there she was cordial.

Well, never let it be said he was the one who gave up the fight. "How's little Curtis doing?" he asked.

"It's like you thought. Fetal alcohol syndrome. He's got a tough life ahead of him but I got him in a program that has some luck treating kids with his disorder. I'll be following him medically. He's a cute little boy."

"I'd be interested in learning more," he said, out of the blue. "Maybe we could get together sometime and you could give me some pointers."

She looked almost taken aback. "Um…sure. Why not?"

"You name the time and place," he said, "and I'll be there."

"Friday night, if I can get a sitter? Or do you have plans?"

He chuckled. "Plans? Me have plans? Not for a long, long time."

"Good, then, Friday it is…" She paused. Frowned.

"Anxiety over leaving the baby behind?"

"Other than my work days it's the first time I'll have left him."

"Well, you need a night away from the kiddies—all of them. Some good old-fashioned adult company. So how about we grab a pizza and you can give me the basic crash course on FAS? I understand you've done some writing on it and presented some lectures."

She shrugged. "I used to, but I'm not inclined to take up my time that way, now. Oh, and we'll have to make it an early evening because I don't want to disrupt Charlie's schedule. In fact, instead of going out for pizza, how about we order in? Then I won't have to get a sitter or disrupt anything."

"A night in with you and…?"

"Charlie. Named after my dad."

"A night in with you and Charlie. Sounds doable."

"Great, come over early, around six. He's usually tired out from day care and ready to go down for a nap for an hour or so. We can have the pizza then. Then after bedtime we'll talk about FAS, if that's OK with your schedule."

She almost sounded excited. It was as if she was starved of adult interaction. She must have been to invite *him* over. Of course, she still wasn't going to get too far away from her baby. There'd been a time when he was like that with Amy. He'd been married to Yvette for six months before knowing of her existence. When Amy's dad had dropped a small child at their door, Simon had immediately stepped into the role of protective father. He'd been the one to feed her, and put her to bed and spend evenings at home with her while Yvette was out running around. He'd been the one to take care of her when she was sick, and take her off to her first day of school. He'd gone to "meet the teachers" night and to the play her first-grade class had put on. Never Yvette. And with that kind of relationship he'd never expected Yvette to simply yank Amy out of his life the way she had. But it was done now, and there was nothing he could say or do to change that. His parenting days were over and, yes, he could understand Del's overprotectiveness because he'd been much the same way.

She reminded him of him, back in happier days. Which was why he resented her. She had what he wanted. But he didn't want it from another one like Yvette, who came equipped with a child already. He wanted his own child next time, one that couldn't be ripped away from him the way Amy had been. "It sounds fine since I don't have anything else to do."

She jotted down her address and gave it to him. "Good. I'll see you then."

"Do you drink wine, or are you…?"

"Nursing? No, I'm not. You can't put your child in the day-care center if he or she's still nursing. So it's strictly the bottle and baby food all the way. And yes, I drink wine. Not much, though, since I work with FAS and I've seen what alcohol can do to a child."

"Then you wouldn't be offended if I bring over a bottle?"

"If you're not offended that I'll have only one glass."

He nodded. "One glass it is." It sounded more like a business transaction than arranging a date, even if it was a working date. So maybe in Del's mind it was a business transaction. Who knew? Admittedly, he was a little disappointed by her attitude, but what had he expected? A real date? They were hardly friends, barely cordial colleagues, and all of a sudden he'd asked her out. Of course, she had a child, which made her safe and he supposed that was part of it. He felt safe with Del because of his personal resolution. So, it wasn't such a bad situation at all. And it would save him from spending another long, dreary night at home alone, looking at pictures of Amy or mulling over how much he missed her.

"Well, he's down for a nap, and the pizza's hot so what say we dig in?" Simon said, pouring himself a glass of wine and leaving the bottle on the table so Del wouldn't feel pressured into drinking if she didn't want to. As it turned out, she poured half a glass and sipped it almost cautiously as they ate their pizza and talked about the clinic. "He's a cute kid," Simon said. "Your Charlie."

"Thank you. I think so, but then I'm a little partial."

"Better that than some of what we see come into the clinic."

"Why did you choose pediatrics?" she asked.

"Liked it when I rotated through when I was an intern. Liked the kids, like the way they're braver than many adults. And they show so much heart and trust. I think it's the vulnerability and trust that got to me. Most adults don't have that. They're cynical, or mistrustful. I remember one patient who told me right off the bat he had the right to sue me if he didn't like the way I treated him and the hell of it was, he had his choices but as an intern I didn't have those same choices, as in not treating him. Luckily his diagnosis turned out to be something simple, but you know the guy never even said thank you. He simply accused me of overcharging his insurance company. Which is one of the reasons I went with children. They're not so vindictive."

"Most adults aren't, either. You just happened to have a bad one at a time in your early career where you were open to influence."

"I gave some thought to going into a straight family practice but I just didn't like treating adults the way I enjoyed taking care of the kids."

"Which is a good reason to go into pediatrics. Family practice's loss."

"Not really a loss so much as I never gave it a fair trial. I'd already decided I wanted to treat children."

"Because you like kids that well?"

"Generally, yes. Says the man who isn't a father."

"You don't have to be a father to be a good pediatrician. All it takes is a passion for what you're doing."

He looked away for a minute, turned deadly serious. "I had this one little guy who was born with cerebral palsy. He wasn't too severe but he had some limitations in walking and coordination, and the way he took to his physical therapy just made me so proud of him. He worked hard, never complained, never questioned. Just did what he was supposed to do when he was supposed to do it and I suppose he was my turning point. I'd always thought I'd be a surgeon, or something a little more showy, but with the kids I found that I liked the courage I saw every day. So I stuck with children and I have no regrets. Now you tell me yours."

"There was never a choice for me. I never had any grand delusions of going into one of the higher profile types of medicine. I liked children, liked working with them, and I think a lot of that stems from my childhood pediatrician, Dr. Dassett. He was a kind man and I was never afraid of going to see him. So even when I was a kid myself I always told my parents I was going to grow up and be just like Dr. Dassett. And here I am."

"But FAS? How did you get interested in that?"

She shrugged. "One of my earliest patients was born with FAS and it interested me that a mother could do that to her child. So, I studied it, and eventually specialized in it." She took a bite of pizza and washed it down with a sip of wine. "I still can't explain the mind that thinks it's OK to do that to your child, but my job is to coordinate care when I get the opportunity. Admittedly, we don't see a lot of that at Lakeside, but I do get called out on referrals to other local hospitals from time to time."

"Isn't it discouraging?" he asked her as he grabbed up his second piece of pizza.

"Very. But somebody has to do it, so why not me? I see all the expectant mothers who drink—it's all just selfishness, or that 'bury your head in the sand' attitude where you think it can't happen to you. And odds are it won't. But occasionally..." She shrugged. "It's one of the ugly sides of medicine, but I can do it and make a difference, which makes me glad I've chosen FAS as my specialty because when you see one of these kids succeed..." She smiled. "If you want pretty you become a beautician. If you want to make a difference you become a doctor. And personally, I've always wondered what's up with someone who wants to practice proctology. Now to me, that's a field of medicine I'd rather not think about."

Simon laughed. "When you put it in those terms, I can kind of agree with you. But for me it's radiology where you don't get much patient contact. I like patients. Like working with them, like curing them or making them feel better, and viewing film and images just isn't what I care to do. Although the world certainly does have need of great radiologists, especially in so many of the specific treatments and tests that get referred to them. Most everything starts with an X-ray of some sort, I suppose, but I can't see myself in that role."

"So do you like Chicago?" she asked. "Is that why

you applied here? Or were you just looking to get away from Boston and Chicago is where you were accepted?"

"I'm from Chicago originally and I wanted to get back here. Had that little hiccup called marriage back in Boston when I was finishing my residency, which didn't make moving home too practical since my wife was born and raised in Boston and wouldn't leave there for me, even though I begged her. So I had to be the flexible one. And then she moved to Chicago anyway, so I did, too. It's nice to come home to the big city. Not that Boston is small, but I love the lakeshore here, which is where I grew up, love the Navy Pier and all the park along the river." He smiled. "It's nice to be back where I belong. So are you from here?"

"South side. Some people call it Indiana, but once you get past Merrillville, which is where I'm from, it all turns into Chicago whether or not it really is. I love a happening city. Love the restaurants, the theater, the museums. And like you I'm hooked on the lakeshore. I can't wait until Charlie's old enough to go to the Museum of Science and Industry, or take a ride on the Navy Pier Ferris wheel. I've got big plans for him. Already have him enrolled in a private school for when he's old enough."

"Well, the coincidence is, we live only a block apart. And I was raised three blocks from here. So who says you can never go home? Because I have and I'm glad to be here."

"Are your parents here?"

"Same condo building I was raised in. They love

it, too, although now that they're older they winter in Florida."

"My parents vacationed in Costa Rica and loved it so much they stayed. Now with Charlie, though, they come back every couple of months, which is good because he's really the only family they have."

"No brothers or sisters?"

She shook her head. "Just me. And you?"

"One brother, who's also a doctor, and a sister, who's a military surgeon."

"Your parents wouldn't happen to be doctors, would they?"

"My dad was a surgeon, my mom was a teacher."

"And they both worked and raised you kids at the same time?"

He nodded. "It worked out."

"My parents were both practicing physicians. My mother has had fits with me now that I've chosen to have a baby and work at the same time, which is what she did. She wants me to stay home with Charlie, and they'll help me out financially if I need it. First grandchild and all."

"Doesn't sound like a bad deal," he said, taking his third slice of pizza.

"But it's not my deal. I want it all, and that includes my job. Speaking of wanting it all, I hear someone stirring in his crib. Sounds like it's bath and snack time for Charlie."

"Does he like it?" Simon teased.

"Give him time." She hopped up and went to get

Charlie, then brought him out to see Simon. "Want to hold him while I get his snack ready?" she asked.

"Sure," he said, but reluctantly. He stretched out his arms to take the bundle from Del as she got a jar of smooshed bananas ready for Charlie. Then when she took him back the baby giggled in anticipation of what he knew was coming.

"He loves his bananas," she said, putting him in his high chair. "Everything but vegetables. He spits out anything that's green."

"Smart kid. Vegetables..." He turned up his nose. "Not a big fan myself unless they're on my pizza."

Snack time was finished, then came bath time, play time and bedtime story, and Charlie was ready to crash for the night. Or at least part of the night. So she put him down and came back out to the living room only to find that Simon was cleaning up the kitchen mess Charlie had made. "You don't have to do that. He hasn't got the finesse of fine dining down yet so half of everything goes on the floor."

"What's a few spilt bananas among the boys?" he asked, laughing. "Besides you look tired and I thought some help might be welcomed."

"Help is always welcomed, but I thought you wanted to talk FAS."

"Not tonight, Del. I've had a nice evening so why ruin it with something so serious?"

"In that case I might be up to another half glass of wine before you leave, if you don't mind."

"Want to keep the bottle?"

She shook her head. "Drinking alone is sad. Even if it is wine."

"Which is why I never drink alone," he replied. "It doesn't go with cold cereal anyway."

"Cold cereal?" she asked as he wrung out the wash-rag and placed it on a drying rack inside the sink cabinet door.

"My usual evening fare. Unless I stop and take something home with me like Chinese or Thai. Trust me, eating is not high on my priority list."

"But you don't look emaciated."

He laughed. "I'm not emaciated. I just have bad eating habits. Besides, I usually have a pretty good lunch at the hospital. The doctors' cafeteria is fairly respectable."

"What about a home-cooked meal?"

"What's that?" he asked.

"What I'm going to cook for you Sunday night if you don't have other plans. I'm not a gourmet chef by a long shot but I do love to cook, and I've been practicing for the time when Charlie starts to eat real food. So, dinner?"

"You sure you want to do this?"

She nodded. "I'm working tomorrow, but I'm off Sunday, so I think I can whip up something you'll like and maybe we can talk FAS then."

"What time?"

"How about eight o'clock, after Charlie's down for the first part of the night?"

"He doesn't sleep through the night yet?"

"He's rambunctious. And eager to get up and play. What can I say? He's all boy."

"And you indulge that?"

"I embrace it." She smiled. "Love it, too, even if the clinic staff has to suffer my grumpiness the next day."

"So now I'll know why to stay away from you on the days you look frazzled."

She shrugged. "I've enjoyed our evening, Simon. You're very considerate, actually. Better than what I expected."

"You were expecting an ogre?"

"Not so much as a grouch."

"Well deserved."

"But you're not really a grouch, either. Just someone who's preoccupied."

"Not so preoccupied as grumpy."

"Why?"

"I had a daughter, Amy. Stepdaughter, actually. Raised her from being tiny and when her mother and I divorced, I lost the battle. She had a restraining order taken out on me. I can't see her, or talk to her. When I'm grumpy that's usually what it's about."

"Simon, I'm so sorry. I didn't… Can't even imagine…"

"Most of the time I still can't imagine it, either. But it is what it is and so far there's been nothing I can do about it."

"You've gone to court?"

"Several times without any luck. Yvette says no, that my presence wrecks her little family and she doesn't want me around. So I'm excluded."

"I wish I knew what to say or do."

"So do I, but the battle is over and I lost." He shrugged. "And Amy's the one left to suffer."

"I can't even imagine what I'd do if someone took Charlie from me."

"You'd let it tear you up. You wouldn't sleep, or eat. You'd walk around in a blur."

She corked the wine bottle and handed it to him. "So you would consider coming over Sunday night for dinner?"

"Looking forward to it," he said, taking the bottle of wine from her. "My days off get lonely."

The brush of his smooth hand across hers gave her goose bumps. Luckily, she was in long sleeves and he couldn't see them, but she could surely feel them skipping up and down her arms. "Good night, Simon."

"Good night, Del," he replied, then headed to the front door of her condo. It was on the twenty-first floor overlooking the lake, and she wondered since he lived only a block away if it also overlooked his condo. But she didn't ask. Didn't want to be tempted. Didn't want to catch herself going to the window and gazing out wondering if he was gazing back.

It was physical attraction, that was all. But she did like him better than she had before this evening. In fact, she liked him a lot. If only Eric had been this nice to be with she might not have left him, but he'd been a bully. Never lifted a finger to help, always criticized, and most of all he always cheated and lied afterward. Somehow, she didn't see those ugly traits in Simon. In fact, now that she knew him a little better personally, she had an idea he was full of good traits. Except for his grumpy days, but now she knew what that was about and felt bad for him.

Del frowned as she put Charlie to bed. Life was good to her. Very good. She was glad for what she had.

CHAPTER THREE

SATURDAY WAS BUSY and complicated after her first non-date date with Simon. They had time to catch a quick lunch in the doctors' cafeteria but she missed out on Charlie's lunch altogether. She felt guilty about that but there was nothing she could do because work came first.

"You OK?" Simon asked her that afternoon.

"I miss Charlie. I hate not being there for his lunch."

"I'm sure he won't notice."

"I think he will. It's part of his routine now. And I'm sure he misses it."

"Babies are forgiving at that age. Take him to the park or something on his way home. I know it's getting chilly out so his outside days to play are numbered until spring. In fact, take off work now and I'll cover for you."

"Do you mean that?" she asked excitedly.

"Of course I mean it. Take Charlie out and go have some fun."

She was taken aback by Simon's generosity. And to think her first impressions were that he was grumpy. Yet he was the furthest thing from ill-tempered she could think of. "You're sure?"

"It's a beautiful day. We're not busy for once. Go take advantage."

Stirred by the moment, Del reached up and kissed him on the cheek. "Thank you. You don't know how much this means to me."

"Yes, I do," he whispered in return as she sped to her office to grab her jacket. "I really do."

The afternoon couldn't have gone more perfectly. They played in the park, stopped at the pier for dinner and ice cream and went home exhausted. By the time the doorman buzzed them in, Charlie was sound asleep, his face covered with chocolate.

"Looks like you two had a big afternoon," he said.

Del smiled.

"We did. Sort of a gift from a friend."

"He must be a good friend."

"Getting to be." More than she'd ever anticipated.

"Well, have a pleasant evening. And tell Charlie he looks good in a chocolate moustache."

Laughing, she caught the elevator and rode all the way up thinking of Simon for most of the ride. She was looking forward to fixing dinner for him tomorrow night, which made her wonder what these growing feelings for him were all about…

CHAPTER FOUR

"I WASN'T SURE what the proper etiquette was so I brought flowers." Simon handed Del a spray of white and red carnations at the door before he entered her condo. "Hope nobody here's allergic to them." Truth was, they were a last-minute detail. He knew it was appropriate to bring a hostess gift like a bottle of wine, but she'd take months to drink the whole thing and it would turn to vinegar in the meantime, so flowers were second on his go-to list, not that he'd ever bought flowers for anyone before. But for Del, and all her feminine ways, they seemed appropriate.

"They're lovely," she said, taking the flowers from him and stepping back to let him in. "You really didn't have to, Simon, but I'm glad you did."

He wondered for a moment if the gesture was too romantic, as he clearly didn't want to shoot that intention out there. Sure, Del was drop-dead gorgeous, and she was actually very nice when they were getting along. But now he worried if the flowers signaled something more than a thank-you for the dinner tonight. "Well, my mother taught me it was customary to take a hostess gift and…"

"And you had a very conscientious mother."

"She insisted on all things done properly and I can almost hear her berating me for skipping a hostess gift."

"Well, flowers are perfect. They brighten up the place." She dug out a vase from under the sink, filled it with water and put the flowers in it, then set the flowers on the kitchen table. "Sorry, but I don't have a formal dining room here. When I bought the place I never anticipated having someone else living here with me, so I sort of low-balled my expectations of what I wanted in my living space. But I'm going to have to upgrade to something larger pretty soon to make room for the both of us, especially when Charlie gets a little older."

"I have too much space. Don't know what I was thinking when I bought it but I've got enough space to host an army. Bought the condo back in the days when I'd anticipated having some visitation privileges with Amy. Unfortunately, that never happened. So I've thought about downsizing but what's the point? I'm settled here and it's as good a place to stay as any."

"Well, if you ever decide to sell, keep me in mind. I figure I've got about two more years here, if that long. Oh, and I want to stay in the neighborhood. I love the lakeshore." She showed him to the kitchen table, where he took a seat and she poured him a glass of wine.

"You bought that for me?"

"It goes with dinner…lasagna and salad."

He smelled the delicious meal cooking. "How did you know Italian is my favorite?"

"Because Italian's everybody's favorite, isn't it?" she said, laughing as she pulled lasagna from the oven and popped in a loaf of garlic bread.

"Did you ever think about moving away from here… from Chicago?" he asked as he poured a glass of wine about one-third full.

"I had offers. Still get them because of my specialty. But I like it fine just where I am and don't feel inclined to uproot myself and Charlie just to take another job. And you? Now that you're back home, is it for good, or can other bright lights tempt you away?"

"You know what they say about Chicago. Once you were born and raised there it will eventually call you back home. I'm home this time. Nowhere to go. And nothing else particularly interests me. Came back when Yvette moved Amy here and I don't feel inclined to move away."

"We're just a couple of old fuddy-duddies stuck in our ways, aren't we?" she asked.

If only she knew how stuck he was. Simon raised his glass and clinked it to hers. "Here's to a couple of old fuddy-duddies."

"Fuddy-duddies," she repeated, then laughed. "Although I wouldn't say thirty-five is old."

"Your wisdom is, though."

"Why, Doctor, I think you just paid me a compliment whether or not you intended to."

Oh, he'd intended to. Del was wise beyond her years. And so settled into her life. He envied her that, in a way. Of course, there'd been a time when he'd thought he'd been settled into his own ways and look how that had turned out! Disastrous, pure and simple. That was his one and only mistake, though. Next time he'd know better.

"I meant to," he said. "You've accomplished so much in so few years, and now you're a successful mom. That's an amazing life no matter how you look at it, Del."

"Well, you're not so shabby yourself. I read where you were the head of your clinic and you gave it all up to come back home and take a lesser position just so you could be back in Chicago."

"I'll advance again. I'm not worried about that. And even if I don't, I like where I am."

"Are you sure, Simon? It seems to me that you prefer bigger challenges than we can give you."

"I'll admit I miss the challenge, but this is fine. It gets me exactly where I want to be." Closer to Amy.

"But you're not committed to staying with us if something better comes along?"

"We'll talk about that if and when we need to. Until then, how about we eat? I'm starved for that lasagna."

Dinner turned out to be a pleasant affair, from the salad course right down to the tiramisu she'd fixed for dessert. They talked about their childhoods and compared neighborhoods and schools, discussed families and friends. Avoided work and life goals pretty much altogether. And before he knew it dinner was over and he was stuck in the odd place on whether to extend the evening by staying on a little longer or going right home. Charlie took care of that problem, though, as he awoke and started crying.

"Look, you take care of the baby and I'll see myself out," he said.

"You don't have to leave," Del replied. "It'll only take me half an hour or so to get him to go back to sleep."

"He's the priority, Del, and I don't want you rushing him through a routine he needs just because you feel guilty neglecting me. So, I'll go, and see you at work tomorrow."

"I'll bring leftovers for lunch," she said.

Was that an invitation to lunch? "Sounds good to me," he said, not at all sure what her intention was. Maybe she'd just hand him a bowl of lasagna and go on her merry way, or there was the possibility they'd sit together and enjoy a leisurely lunch. Whatever the case, he wasn't comfortable asking, so instead he walked over to Del, gave her a tender kiss on the cheek and thanked her for the evening. "It's nice to get out for a change."

"You don't date?" Del asked Simon as he headed toward the front door.

"Nope. Too soon. The wound hasn't healed enough and I'm generally not that trusting of relationships right now." If ever again.

"Too bad because I think you'd make a terrific date for someone. Maybe you'll meet someone in the clinic or the hospital."

Except he wasn't looking, as most of the women who fell into his age category had children and he wasn't going to do that to himself again. He'd been hurt badly the first time and he wasn't going to do that again. "Thanks again for the evening," he said, then disappeared out the front door.

* * *

"He's different, Charlie," she said as she laid her baby back down in his crib. "He seems like he'd be a great candidate for someone to date, yet he won't date. Maybe his divorce hit him harder than I assumed it did. But the thing is, I don't think he's even looking for companionship. He seems happy being single."

Charlie looked up at her and giggled.

"Well, I'm glad you think it's funny. But mark my words, one of these days you're going to be out there looking and it's not going to be easy finding the right one. Just look at the mess your mommy made of her life for five years. That should teach you something."

Five years of bullying and verbal abuse and she hadn't gotten out of it quickly enough. But she'd lived in the hope that Eric would change at some point, not that he ever had. It had forced her to change, though. Forced her out on her own into the world, where she'd had no choice but to make it all by herself. Surprisingly, she'd discovered she liked it that way. Liked everything about it including her notion to get inseminated and have a baby on her own, owing to her biological clock ticking and all that. Her doctor had told her time was running out for her. Her ovaries were beginning to fizzle out. No, she wasn't too old to have a baby yet, and that was still a ways off, but she hadn't wanted to put it off any longer since she really intended on having a brother or sister for Charlie somewhere down the road.

So one year from her breakup date she'd embarked on a new adventure and she'd loved every minute of it from the pregnancy to the birth. Having Charlie was the single best thing she'd ever done and she didn't regret even a moment of it.

Charlie reached his hands up for her to hold him and, while she normally didn't give in to his little stall tactics, tonight she wanted to feel him in her arms. "OK, so you win just this once but don't think your mommy's going to be a pushover all the time, because it's not going to happen." Although it was happening more and more now that she was working and leaving him behind. "He's a nice man, though, Charlie. Just like yesterday when he covered so we could have time in the park together. I'll admit that Simon and I got off on the wrong foot but that seems to be behind us now."

She hoped so, anyway. Because she really liked him and could even fancy herself dating him sometime. Not that she intended for *that* to happen. But it was caught up in her daydreams. So she pushed it aside and sang Charlie one of his favorite little songs. *Down in the meadow by the itty, bitty pool…*as she glanced at the bouquet of flowers and smiled. Honest to goodness, this was the first time anybody had ever given her flowers and it made her feel special.

"Room Three has an advanced case of bronchitis," she said in greeting to Simon the next morning. "Room Two has a broken arm—just a greenstick fracture, I think. We're waiting for X-rays. And Room One has a little girl who's just started having periods and she has the cramps. So take your pick."

"Good morning to you," he said, looking up on the sign-in board. There were six other cases signed in to various other doctors. "Looks like today's going to be a busy one."

"It happens," she said, giving him a big smile.

"Then I'll start with the bronchitis and work my way down. How's that sound?"

"I'll take the cramps," Del volunteered. "At age eleven I think she'll be more at ease with a female doctor."

They parted ways and Simon went to have a look at his bronchitis patient, a little boy named Bart. He was eight. "How long have you been sick?" he asked Bart.

"Three days," his mother answered. "At first we thought it was a cold."

"Well, we'll get that fixed right up for you. Give you some medicine and send you home to rest. And you'll be up and around inside five or six days."

"Thank you," his mother said. "I was so afraid it would be something worse." She brushed a tear off her cheek. "I don't know what I'd do if he got really sick."

"You'd bring him here and we fix him up."

"It not easy being a single mother…no one there to help me through it."

"I can imagine how hard that is." Simon gave Bart a shot and a prescription and sent them on their way. Thinking about Amy in the intermittent seconds.

"Cute kid," Del said in passing.

"Mom's single. Having a rough time of it. No support." He sighed. "I told her I knew how hard that could be."

"You've got great empathy, Simon. Being a single

mom without having support's got to be the hardest thing in the world. I'm lucky I've got all kinds of support."

"I learned to be empathetic and not to judge after I became a pediatrician."

"It's good that you care so deeply. I mean, word eventually got around when I was pregnant and I lived some pretty rocky months where I heard things like, *'She's a doctor, she should have known better.'* And, *'She's a doctor, how could she be a good example to our older patients?'*

"It hurt, Simon, and I'd be lying if I said it didn't. But it was my choice not to tell anybody the circumstances at the time because that would have only brought on more speculation and rumors. So I gritted my teeth and worked through it."

He admired her for her convictions and knew she was right. But he still thought of Amy and Yvette and wondered what kind of support Amy got from her mother.

He'd always been the better parent to that child, and it hurt him thinking what situation Amy might be living in now. But there was nothing he could do about it, just as there was nothing he could do to convince Yvette to allow him to have more time with Amy.

Yvette certainly wasn't abusive, more like negligent, but she'd be the type who put off an illness for too long, or sign away permission to a virtual stranger. She certainly wouldn't have been worried the way Del would be, or Bart's mother. Maybe those thoughts were where all his angst was coming from. Then to look at Del and see what kind of a super mother she was...that just made him angrier thinking how Amy deserved something like that.

"You're one in a million, Del," he said. "A lady with strong convictions who puts up with the ridicule simply to get what she wants. I admire that in you."

"Thanks," she said.

"Anyway, I'm going to run over to the hospital to check on some patients. Got a couple I'm worried about." And getting his mind back on work would take it off Yvette.

"That's nice of you, Simon. I like it when a doctor goes above and beyond the call of duty."

The more she got to know him, the more she liked him. He was certainly unique to their staff in the way he cared. And she didn't even mind that gruffness in him. Most of it was justified considering the situation with his stepdaughter.

She wondered how long someone with his talent would stay around, though. Amy might move somewhere else. Or he'd have other offers. Offers better than any they could do for him. In fact, she could see him in charge of a hospital pediatrics department, he was so authoritative. That was what worried her. She liked having him here, liked his skill, and as far as she was concerned he was on the open market for something better. Well, it was one of those bridges she'd have to cross when she got to it, she supposed.

"Well, all my patients are doing fine," Simon said, strolling down the hall. "And everyone is happy. So what's next on the board?"

"Twins. Both with runny noses and fevers. Aged two. And a mother who definitely frets to the point of obsession."

"Good," he said, grabbing the chart off the stack, then heading down to Exam Five, where he found two-year-old twins, both with simple colds, and a mother who was worried to death. With all the worrying he'd been doing over Amy lately, it was nice seeing a good mother. It restored his faith in humanity.

"The lasagna is in the fridge with your name on it. Eat as much as you'd like. In the meantime I'm going to run next door and see Charlie. He's expecting me."

Admittedly, Simon was a little disappointed, but not surprised that she preferred to spend her lunch hour with her son. In fact, he would have been surprised if she hadn't. "Have a nice lunch hour," he said.

"Any time I'm with Charlie is nice," she replied as she trotted toward the front door of the clinic. Unfortunately, one of her patients walked in at the same time she was leaving and she had no recourse but to see the child. So she had the girl checked in and spent the next thirty minutes with her, only to send her over to the hospital for an appendectomy. By then it was too late to go see her son but Simon was on his way over there to check on a couple of patients so she stepped into the men's locker room to ask him to check on Charlie for her.

"Simon," she called out to him, admiring the lines of his body in the transparent curtain.

"Care to join me?" he teased.

She liked the contours of his lean body. And yes, even doctors could admire. Which she did. Immensely.

"Since I didn't go over there at lunch and he'll be going down for his afternoon nap any time, I was wondering if you might check in on Charlie for a minute to make sure he's OK."

"Sure," he called, then stepped out of the shower with nothing but a towel wrapped around him. "Now, you can either stay and watch me dress, which I wouldn't mind because I'm not really shy, or you can leave. Your choice." He grinned. "Want to think about it for a couple minutes? I'll be glad to wait." He adjusted his towel a little tighter around his mid-section so it wouldn't accidentally fall.

"Sorry," she mumbled, then backed out the door, leaving him laughing as she exited.

"I am a doctor," she said, as he left the locker room a few minutes later all scrubbed and fresh and ready to go. "It's not like I haven't seen a naked man before."

"But you haven't seen *this* naked man, not that he cares. But people might talk, especially if someone walked in on us while I was still naked," Simon said, coming up behind her.

Del blushed. "I wasn't thinking."

"I was," he said, grinning. "And it's been a while since I caused a lady to blush the way you are right now."

"But I didn't mean to...well, you know. Come gawking. All I wanted to do was ask you to look in on Charlie for me."

"Which I'll be glad to do." These were the words to

which he departed and surprisingly, ten minutes later, Del got a short movie texted to her phone. It was Charlie, who was fast asleep, looking all innocent only the way a baby could. She texted Simon back to thank him, and saved the movie in case, well, she wasn't sure why since she'd see her baby in another few hours. But she was so touched by the gesture she didn't have the heart to get rid of it. And over the next hour, while Simon was at Lakeside checking in on various kids, she couldn't count the number of times she replayed that ten seconds' worth of video, thinking not only of Charlie but of Simon when she did.

"I've almost worn out the video," Del said as Simon walked through the clinic's front door. "Thank you so much for doing that for me."

"No big deal," he said. "I was there and it didn't disturb Charlie, so what the hell? I decided one video was worth a thousand words."

"Or more," she said, standing up on her tiptoes and giving him a kiss on the cheek.

He blushed and backed away. No way was he going to become that involved with Del, so he wasn't going to let it start even in the simple gestures. "What's up next?" he asked uncomfortably.

"A couple cases of the croup, an advanced case of diaper rash and a general physical. Take your pick."

"I'll start with the diaper rash," he said and grabbed up the chart and headed down to Exam Four. "Good afternoon," he said on his way in the door. "I'm Dr.

Michaels, and I understand someone here has a persistent case of diaper rash."

"I've tried everything," the mother said. She looked worn out. "And nothing works."

"Well, take off Angela's diaper and I'll have a look."

Outside in the hall, Del stood and watched the door behind which Simon was treating a baby. She sighed. No, she wasn't in the mood to get involved with anyone, but another time, another place, and it might have been him. Except he seemed as uninterested as she did. So it was a no go all the way around. But he surely would have been a great dad for Charlie, if she'd been in the daddy-hunting business.

Except she wasn't.

"Too bad," she whispered as she walked away. Yep, too, too bad.

CHAPTER FIVE

IT WASN'T THAT she needed the company; wasn't even so much that she wanted it. But when Simon asked her and Charlie out for dinner she found it hard to turn him down. He understood the restrictions, too. Home by seven thirty so she could go through her evening routine with her son. Bath time, bedtime story, a little song, then sit with him until he was fast asleep. It was a routine that really didn't give her much time for a normal social life for herself, but that was fine and dandy with her. This was all she needed in her after-work hours. "I need to stop and pick up some diapers," she told Simon, before he followed her home in his car so he could drive them on their date for three. "And some baby food, if you don't mind waiting."

"I'll be glad to go with you—that way you won't have so much to carry."

"Would you?" she asked. "I'd appreciate that." Suddenly, she found herself looking forward to their abbreviated evening together. It had been a long time since she'd had a real date and while this was not so traditional, it was real enough that she was excited to get out for a little while. Life with Charlie was fulfilling, but she did miss adult companionship outside of work sometimes. So they made a quick stop at the grocery store, then she took her car home and changed clothes, changed Charlie and was back out and ready to go in a matter of minutes. In the meantime, Simon had fixed the baby's car seat in the backseat of his car just as if he knew what he was doing.

"Tell me about Boston," she said as they entered the restaurant. "Did you like it?"

"I loved it. It's such a historic town, so picturesque. And so expensive. I had to rent a parking space outside my town house that cost me fifty thousand a year. And I had to walk a block to get to it. By most standards that's obscene but that was part of the charm living in a Boston town house."

"That's why I like Chicago. It may be large but it's not inconvenient. And I love all the services and sights here. And the fact that in most areas you get parking to go along with your condo. It's all included in the price of the unit."

"I like that, too, and that's one of the reasons why I came back. Home is where the heart is, and this is home to me." The heart, and Amy.

"Do you ever miss Boston?"

"Some, but I miss Amy more." He sighed. "And you?"

"I was in Indianapolis with Eric for a while before he was in medical school. During our last year of medical school I'd already decided I wanted my own life, no outside interference from anybody. Eric and I were actually estranged the last year we were together, only it was just easier to ignore it. But I'd started making plans for when he was gone, and having a baby was part of it. Charlie wasn't an afterthought, but more like a sign of my independence." She smiled wistfully as she gave him a bite of food. "He's part of my liberation...the best part because I really did want him so badly, and my lack of relationship had nothing to do with it. And of course, the clock was also ticking.

"You're not that old."

"I didn't want to be that old when I had him, either. So I made the decision and stuck by it.

"Good for you," he said, picking up the baby spoon and giving Charlie another bite to eat.

It came so naturally to him, she thought. Just like the baby seat. It must have been looking after Amy. It was as if he was meant to have a child of his own. Of course maybe it was the pediatrician coming out in him, too.

"Well, it's nice being on my own. I was a mess at first, right after the breakup, and I almost gave in a couple times when he begged me to take him back. He promised to change. But he had habits that don't change so easily, like those other women in his life. And after all those years I found out he didn't even want children. He knew I did. I'd talked about it, told him I couldn't wait until we started to have our family, and he always said one day we would. Then I caught him cheating, and who wants to bring a child into that situation?"

"You knew he was cheating?"

"I suspected for a while, but I was afraid to confront him because I didn't want to know. That was me with my 'head buried in the sand' phase. Once I pulled it out, though, I discovered just how much was out there that I'd missed, and how much I was going to miss if I continued to hold on to him. My baby being the biggest thing. I wanted one so badly…" She brushed a tear from her eye. "So, did your ex cheat on you?" she asked him.

He shook his head. "She was faithful as far as I know. Just bored because she didn't bargain on a doctor keeping a doctor's hours. And back in Boston I worked pediatrics in the ER, which kept me pretty busy most of the time. So when she started complaining, I took a job in a clinic, but I still had long hours as I was the director and I didn't get the eight-to-five job she thought I'd get. Then there were my on call hours, hospital rounds…it was a busy job and she simply got tired of sitting around waiting for me to come home. So one day I came home to divorce papers and that's all there was."

"Did you love her?"

"I loved the idea of her, but I fell out of love with her because of all her nagging. I had a job to do and she never could understand that I was busy. So, after the divorce, she remarried someone who could give her all the attention she needed."

"You sound bitter."

"Maybe I am. She certainly surprised me without any kind of warning. Married one day and on my way to a divorce the next. It was a shock, to say the least."

"I'll bet it was," Del said, noticing that Charlie was nodding off. "And on that note, I think we need to call it a night." Too bad, too, as she was enjoying herself with

Simon. It was good getting to know a little more about him, and telling him about her. Although there was still something she couldn't put her finger on. Something deeper in Simon that he wasn't talking about. About Amy? About the deep pain he went through when he lost her? She could see it in his eyes, hear it in his voice. Sense it in the way he wrung his hands as he looked as if he were a million miles away.

Still, in spite of it all, she liked him. He was a good doctor, which was where it started, and good with Charlie, too, which, for her, was where it all ended. Right now she was simply too frightened to get involved again. It didn't mean she never would, but not now. Not until she worked it around her head that she had it in her to trust completely another man. Not just for her sake now, but for Charlie's, too. He counted in all this. In fact, he counted in a big way.

"Why don't you bring Charlie and come to my place tonight?" he asked on their next day off together. "I'm a fair to good cook and I can make something Charlie will like."

"You really don't mind me bringing Charlie?" She wasn't sure why she was on the verge of accepting, but she was. Maybe it was because she enjoyed his company, or just needed an adult social situation. But she was tipped toward accepting.

"Not at all. He's a cute kid. Good manners for six months."

"We'd love to come." Well, there she'd done it. Gone and accepted.

Which left her in the same spot as she'd been in before. Getting involved where she didn't belong.

Simon smiled, but he also sighed. Maybe it wasn't what he really needed, either, wasn't where he needed to be. But they were growing closer and she liked him. So what did a little dinner again among friends matter anyway? It wasn't as if this were a date, and she wasn't going to let this turn into anything but two friends having dinner together. That much was for sure. Nothing but dinner. End of story. Yet she worried about that, too. So why did she worry so much?

"Why did I do this, Charlie?" she asked as she got the infant ready for his night out. "I invited him, which is bad enough, but then I accepted his invitation, which was even worse. I like the man, but not in the way I should be dating him. Or doing something that could vaguely be construed as a date."

One bad long-term relationship was enough to make her swear off all relationships for quite some time and concentrate on the only man in her life she truly loved—Charlie.

"Momma's going to get this right," she told her son, who was busy playing with a stuffed teddy bear as she tried to dress him. "I promise you, I'm not going to do anything stupid like get involved with Simon. You'd like him and, as a matter of fact, I like him, too, but now's not the right time for that. And I'm not sure if or when there's going to be a right time."

However, who said they couldn't be friends? She'd settle for that and be very happy with the outcome, as she didn't have that many friends on which to count—thanks to Eric, who had been so controlling she'd lost contact with most of her friends from medical school—and she felt as if she could count on Simon. But men always wanted to take it to the next level, and she surely wasn't ready for that. No way, no how.

"Your momma just wants an adult friendship," she said to Charlie, who'd tossed his teddy to the end of his crib and started squiggling around trying to get it. "Which you'll probably never understand since you're going to grow up to be a man. But the truth is, it's not always about sex. Sometimes it's about a close relationship that can include everything that goes along with a good friendship and nothing more. I like Simon that way."

Although, who was she kidding? He was her type, at least physically. In fact, she'd picked out a man with Simon's features to father her child... She liked her men dark, with broad shoulders and green eyes, which fit Simon to a T. A trait she noticed over and over throughout the evening.

"Your cooking's very good," she said as she ate her Chinese stir-fry. "I hope I can teach Charlie to cook when he's older. There's always something appealing about a man who can cook."

"I'm not that good, but I do have a few specialties, so after you've been here four or five times you're going to have to settle for reruns or eat some of my more dubious dishes."

Was he implying four or five more invitations? Suddenly, that gave her very cold feet as it sounded like a dating relationship to her. And just after she'd convinced herself she could be friends with him. Del sighed. What was she getting herself into? "You do realize I don't date, don't you?" she said, being brutally honest with him lest he got ideas about the two of them.

"Neither do I, so that makes us even," Simon replied, then took a bite of the chicken in the stir-fry. "Haven't since my divorce and I don't intend to for a good long time, at least not in the dating sense. It's too rough getting involved then uninvolved."

"So we're OK with this, whatever it is?"

He chewed, then swallowed. "A few meals here and there, maybe a walk in the park…I am if you are. I'm thirty-six and one marriage at my age is enough. I've still got the battle scars to prove it."

"I have some of those myself." She laughed. "So we're both at the same points in our lives, it seems."

"Friendship. No dating. That sounds about right to me."

"But can that work?" she asked. "Because I honestly don't know. I've never been in this position before."

"There's only one way to find out," he answered. "We'll try it until we know one way or another."

"And no one gets hurt?"

"No one gets hurt."

In an ideal world that could work, but she knew they weren't living in an ideal world. They'd both had bad breakups and were gun-shy. Neither one wanted permanence. Well, she'd see. She'd just see what happened. Nothing ventured…

* * *

The evening hung on nicely. They ate, Charlie dozed off, and Del and Simon talked about various medical issues, including FAS. Then all too soon it was over and it was time to take Charlie home and put him to bed.

"Let me walk you," Simon offered. "It's not that far and it is dark outside now."

"I'd appreciate that," she said as she slipped Charlie into his coat and hat.

"It's hard to imagine how close we live and yet we've never bumped into each other on the street."

"I haven't gone out much," she said. "My whole life's been tied up with taking care of Charlie. It hasn't been easy doing it alone so I don't get out too much." She shrugged. "I'm not complaining. Just telling you the facts. Single parenting is difficult and I wouldn't trade it for anything in the world. So if I passed you on the street, nine times out of ten I'd be preoccupied with Charlie and wouldn't even see you." She smiled. "That's just the way it goes."

"I suppose it is. But since I'm not a parent..."

"You'd make a great father," she said, slipping her hand into his. "To any child." As they walked in sync, she could hear him sigh.

"The problem is the one I *want* to be a parent to isn't available to me."

She stopped and held onto him. "You'll work it out. One way or another you'll work it out. I have all the confidence in the world in you, Simon. You're meant to be that little girl's daddy and it will happen."

"All the confidence in the world?"

"Since I've gotten to know you better I do. You're a strong man and a caring one and it will happen for you one of these days. I'm sure of it."

"I'm glad we get along now. You're the strong one, Del. And you say the right words—the words I need to hear to give me hope."

She started to walk again, her hand still in his. "We can be strong in this together for each other. I need someone there to be strong for Charlie and me, and you need someone there strong for you and Amy."

"Equal in strength," he said.

"And needy in a way. It's nice to have someone to rely on."

"You'll make a great parent to your own child one day," she said as she put Charlie in the baby carriage. "When the right woman comes along…"

"You didn't wait," he said to her.

"Biologically, men can produce children much longer than women can. And my time was running out. Besides, I always wanted a child. Eric promised me we'd have one when the time was right, but there was never a right time for him because then he backed out on his promise when he found someone else. So I just decided to do it on my own. No fuss, no muss, no bother. Have my baby by myself and skip all that came in between like the role of the father. Made it easy that way. At least for me."

"But what will you tell Charlie someday?"

"The truth. When he's old enough to understand it."

"Don't you think that will hurt him?" he asked as

they strolled down the street in the direction of Del's condo.

"Not if I do it the right way. He'll understand that he was my choice and not my obligation."

"You're sure of that?"

"If I raise my child the right way, I am. I'll just let him know he was a wanted child and not an accident."

"I hope that works out for you," he said as they stopped in front of her condo. "But you're a great mom, so I suppose it will."

"Thanks for the compliment. But I'll admit, I've thought about that more than once. It's not going to be easy telling him."

"You'll do the right thing when the time comes, Del. Anyone who loves her child as much as you do is bound to."

"Thanks again." She reached up and placed a tender kiss on his cheek. "Maybe you'll find the right woman soon and we can raise our kids together."

"I'm not looking for the right woman right now. Did that once and that was enough for this part of my life."

Del laughed. "Never say never."

"Well, I'm about as close to never as you can get."

"Don't be so pessimistic. You never know what's going to happen in your life."

"True. But I've pretty well put myself into the no-relationship category for now. And what about you?"

"I think I'm sitting right there next to you. I'm not really interested in finding someone right now. Charlie's enough for me."

"You're lucky to have him."

"I know I am. Which is why I don't want to mess things up and bring in someone else. We're good the way we are."

"But what if you met the *one*?"

"What if *you* met the one?"

He thought about it for a minute. "I suppose that's one of those bridges you cross when you get there."

"And keep your fingers crossed you don't get there."

"Come on now, it's not that bad."

"Oh, it was that bad. And toward the end it got worse when he was cheating on me. It caught me off guard."

"You never expected it?"

"At the time I didn't. But later, when I thought about it, I realized he'd been playing me for a fool for quite a while. Then talk about feeling stupid."

"I guess that's the way I felt, too. Pretty damned dumb. She didn't cheat on me but she sure had another life going. Lied about it, and went through my bank account to do it. But in her defense I was busy looking the other way so I can't blame her for that."

"You'd think they'd be honest about it, though. If you don't want to be in the marriage get out, don't bully your way through it like Eric did our relationship. He could have simply left."

Simon shrugged. "Who knows what goes on with people and why they do what they do?"

"One thing's for sure. I'm going to teach Charlie to be better."

"With you as his mother, Charlie's going to turn out fine."

Del blushed. "I appreciate the compliment. I hope I do well with him." She hoped to heaven she did well. Charlie deserved that from her.

CHAPTER SIX

"I'M GOING TO see Charlie in a couple hours or so. Care to tag along and have lunch with us?" she asked the next day. "He sure does like you."

"Can't," Simon practically snarled. "Too busy."

Where did that come from? "Fine. But if you change your mind…good. I'll call you when I'm ready to go over." She glanced at the clock on the wall. "Charlie eats between eleven and twelve."

"And when do you eat?" he asked.

"Hardly ever when I'm on duty. Don't have enough time."

"Don't wait on my account. I have a lot to do." The sacrifices you make for your kids, he thought to himself. He remembered all the sacrifices he'd made for Amy—the missed meals, the days off work, adjusting his schedule to fit to hers as she got older—none of which had been appreciated by Yvette, yet he hadn't begrudged the child anything.

Charlie held his arms up to his momma and she picked him up and cradled him. As it turned out Simon wasn't able to make it, he was so busy. "He's fixed on something and I don't know what it is, but it's work, and you know that work comes first." Charlie giggled then burped. "And you, of course. You're always first."

She did wish there were something...anything she could do to help Simon, though. She felt so bad for him and she could understand what it would be like ripping your child from your arms because she had Charlie.

Charlie snuggled his head against his mother's shoulder, which indicated to Del that it was time for a nap. "I'll see you after work," she promised him, "or before if I can catch a break for fifteen or twenty minutes."

"He's doing splendidly," Mrs. Rogers said as she watched Del put Charlie down in his designated crib. "Plays with the other babies his age as much as a six-month-old can play, and he's caught on to his routine easily. No separation anxiety. He's really a good little boy, so there's really nothing to worry about."

Del breathed a sigh of relief. "I'm the one who has separation anxiety," she said. "And while you say there's nothing to worry about, I still worry."

"Because you're a good mother."

Maybe she was, but that didn't stop the pit in her stomach from growing every time she saw Charlie in day care. She wanted so badly to stay home with him it hurt. But there was nothing she could do. This was her life and she had to make all the pieces fit together. "Thank you," she said humbly. "But that doesn't make it any easier."

"Well, for what it's worth, it will get easier over time, once you've adjusted to *your* new routine. I've seen too many parents come in here and drop off their kids and be glad to get rid of them. It's refreshing to see a parent who frets so much. But I promise you, he's getting good care, as good as we can give him without being his mother."

"I appreciate that," Del said, bending over the crib to give Charlie a kiss on his chubby cheek even though he was already fast asleep. "And if I get in your way or start making a nuisance of myself, please let me know. I don't want to disrupt things here."

"We have fifty children, half that many workers and volunteer grandmas, and the presence of one more person here isn't going to disrupt a thing. In fact, it's good seeing a parent who wants to be so involved. Currently, we have only about a dozen or so parents who make an effort to have lunch with their children."

"That's surprising," Del said, quite stunned at the low percentage. How could a parent not want to spend as much time with his or her child as possible? "Look, I've got to be going," Del said, giving Charlie one last kiss. "I'll see you later, big boy," she whispered in his ear, then went off to find Simon, who was simply standing in the clinic hall, looking at the patient board.

"So many children, so little time." He gave her a sideways glance. "So how was your lunch with Charlie?"

"He slept through most of it. Seems he had a big morning."

"I'm glad someone did. I spent my lunch hour on the phone with the lawyer fighting for Amy. It seems like that's all I do lately."

"Any progress?"

"He said we can start from the beginning again but he wasn't very optimistic that anything would change. He said I'd need more evidence that Amy's being neglected or mistreated—something new that they haven't seen before."

"Is there anything new?"

"Not that I'm aware of. And since I never get to see her..." He shrugged. "It's hard to tell."

"Would Amy ever call you?"

"If she had access to a phone she might, but they make sure she doesn't have access."

"So you can't just call her?"

He shook his head. "That would only make it worse on her and I don't want to do that."

"Do you want to chat about it?" she said. "I've got fifteen minutes."

They went to the doctors' cafeteria, where they found a secluded corner and sat down, he with his coffee, she with her tea. "Let me make this long story short. Yvette took everything I had—my car, my money, my house. Everything. It was for Amy, she told me. She needed a way to support her, and I let her do it. But like an idiot I discovered she took it all for her new boyfriend. He was a gambler and he was tapped out at the time. I felt so stupid giving up everything, but that's what I did and when I came here I barely had enough money to start over. The condo isn't even mine—it's a rental. My life is practically a rental because I wanted to take care of Amy and as it turned out I was left with nothing. Talk about being stupid."

"That's not being stupid. That's loving someone more than you love yourself and you can't fault a person for that." She took hold of his hand. "If you need more hours…"

"More hours aren't going to fix what ails me, I'm afraid. And it's not the money. It's being gullible to my ex. I didn't expect her to do what she did, especially since it involved Amy. If anything happens to her I don't have the means to take care of her properly."

"I'm so sorry, Simon. I can't even imagine what you're going through."

"I moved back to Chicago, because I love it here, but I was perfectly happy in Boston and would be happy anywhere Amy was. But Yvette and Amy are here now, and I'd hoped…well, let's just say I'd hoped she'd come to her senses one of these days and give me visitation rights."

"And there's nothing else you can do?"

He shook his head. "Not a damned thing. The court has spoken and I suppose I could appeal again but I really don't have a legal leg to stand on since she's not my daughter and Yvette would never allow me to adopt her for fear she'd lose child support from Amy's real father."

"Does he have visitation rights?"

Simon shrugged. "I suppose he does, but all he is to Amy is a name attached to a bad connotation. To Yvette he's a monthly check in the mail, and that's it."

"Maybe her new stepfather is good? Although the fact he's a heavy gambler doesn't really put him in a very good light."

"I'm not judging him, because I haven't met the man, but it's hard for me to picture."

"Maybe if you talked to him he might come around."

"Like he did when he took everything I owned before."

Del sighed heavily. "Would either one of them listen to me?"

"I doubt it. Unless you ante up and pay them. Nothing comes cheap or free wherever they're concerned."

"So they wouldn't be amenable to a civil chat from one of your friends?"

"Nope. It's all about what they can get out of any deal and they know they can't get any more out of me...and there's no reason for you to be involved in this mess."

"And in the meantime?"

"I get by."

"Does this explain your mood?"

"I hope so. Because nothing else does. I was on the phone with my lawyer earlier looking for another way in and he wasn't encouraging. Told me straight up that he'd send me a bill first of the month so we could settle up and call it quits."

Del couldn't even imagine what she'd do if someone usurped her rights with Charlie and took him from her. Someone such as the sperm donor who had changed his mind and wanted visitation or, worse yet, custody. The thought of that made her queasy and she pushed her cup of tea away. "You've got to be kidding!"

"I'm afraid I'm not. He fired me."

"Can he do that?"

"Apparently he can."

"Is there anything I can do?" she asked. "Give you a letter of recommendation or appear somewhere on your behalf?"

"I'm afraid the fight is fought. As the judge so eloquently pointed out, I have no rights whatsoever when it comes to Amy. She's not my child, I didn't adopt her, and all I did was what any for-hire child-care worker would do for her."

"Seriously?" She was shocked by the judge's lack of sympathy for a man who loved a child as if she were his own.

"The hearing lasted ten minutes, the verdict came in instantly. Amy is lost to me forever."

"How old is she?"

"Seven."

"Then she'll have memories of you, so maybe someday…"

"After Yvette does a number on me the way she did on Amy's father, there's not going to be any someday. She trashed Amy's father every chance she could and Amy heard it. Yvette never took care to mind her words around her child and that has to have an effect. And I expect if I keep trying to get back into her life she'll do the same to me. Kids that age are so impressionable, too." He shrugged. "I've exhausted everything I know how to do without hurting Amy, or without involving her. Even my own attorney told me it was time to give up for the sake of the child."

"Why did you marry her if she's so vindictive?"

"I never saw that side of her until we'd been married awhile. Then when it came out, it came out ugly. She looked like a good mother. Amy had everything she needed, mostly thanks to me. But I wasn't enough and she reminded me of that every day. I couldn't provide the life she thought she deserved. And to be honest, I think she'd already set her sights on finding her next victim by the time we'd split, because she went directly into his arms three months later."

"With the man she married?"

Simon nodded. "One and the same."

"Oh, I am sorry."

"So am I. Which is why I thought I'd better tell you the rest of the reason why I get so grumpy sometimes. I miss my daughter and there's nothing I can do about it. I owed you that much. And I know all the psychology behind it, went to a shrink for a little while and got my head straightened around. But it still doesn't take away the sting." He shrugged. "Mixed moods is my diagnosis. The doctor said I'll just have to put up with it because there's nothing I can do to fight against it."

"And Yvette won't even let Amy talk to you on the phone? I can't believe that!"

Simon shook his head. "No. It's totally no contact."

"That's cruel for both you and Amy."

"I can't even imagine what Amy's going through right now."

She let go of his hand. Let go of the smooth feel of his skin and hated to do so, but anyone looking on might misconstrue their hand-holding as something more than lending comfort in a bad situation. "Maybe things will change for you. Be patient. Something will work out. It just has to."

"That's what I keep telling myself. But I'm not counting on it."

"Well, like I said, if there's anything I can do..."

"I appreciate that. But I'm afraid I've run out of options."

"You say they're here in Chicago, though."

He nodded. "Which is one of the reasons I was desperate to come back home. First, because I love it here, but also because I felt more steady fighting for Amy here. And I'm closer in case...well, just in case."

Del glanced at her watch and stood. "I think it's time we'd better be getting back. We're already twenty minutes late. Oh, and, Simon—thanks for telling me. I know it can't have been an easy thing to talk about." Not easy at all, and her heart did go out to him. No wonder he didn't want to get involved in a relationship. It was obvious his first marriage was horrible and he was now taking time out to sort things. That was something she understood well.

The afternoon was uneventful, with a waiting room full of sick kids, none of them serious. Some were the products of over-zealous mothers who thought sniffles equated to something bad, while others were sick with various colds, flu bugs and cuts and sprains. By all counts it was a nice afternoon—nice to not see anybody who was seriously ill, and Del was grateful for it as her mind was fixed on Simon and his mess of a life. Even after he'd told her, she still couldn't believe that a caring mother would completely turn him away from her child. Which meant only one thing. Yvette wasn't a very caring mother. She did everything out of her own selfish gain and didn't care about her daughter enough to reunite her with someone who truly loved her.

It was a very self-serving motive, especially since Simon had no financial obligation to the child. Yet Del bet that Simon had supported her for five years, glad to do so, and if he offered to continue that support now, even though his circumstances were dire, she'd probably let him back in. So devious. "What a rotten thing to do," she said to Charlie as she changed him out of his day-care clothes, gave him a bath and put him in his pajamas. "And there's nothing I can do to help him."

She gave Charlie his dinner and spread his play blanket on the floor, but tonight he was being fussy. Wouldn't eat, didn't want to play. Only wanted to sleep. So she took his temperature to make sure he wasn't coming down with anything, found it to be normal and simply sat in her antique Victorian rocker and rocked him to sleep. Just one of those fussy baby days and they did have them, as everybody did. So she didn't worry as he pulled up his knees, stuck his thumb in his mouth and drifted off into a fitful sleep.

After about fifteen minutes she put him down into his crib and leaned over to kiss him, but he shrugged away from her. "Tired from day care?" she asked. "Did you have a big day?"

He didn't respond to her voice, though. Instead, he simply shut his eyes and ignored her. So she checked him once again to make sure he wasn't sick, but he showed no symptoms of anything serious except being extremely tired, so she turned on the night-light and turned off the overhead light and left the room, leaving his door open a crack lest he should start to cry.

Her mother's intuition was instantly on alert, as was her doctor's intuition since Charlie wasn't acting normal, but so far there was nothing to go on that pointed to him being sick. So she settled down on the living-room couch and picked up a medical journal to read. But for some reason, she was too antsy to stay down so she got back up to do some household chores like laundry and dusting—things she barely had time for these days. In fact, her time was so limited she was giving some thought to hiring a housekeeper to come in a couple days a week. She hadn't decided one way or another, though, as she was still pretty adamant she could do it all. Even though all of it was not getting done as much as it had before she'd gone back to work.

On impulse, she called Simon's number and felt silly when he picked up on the second ring. "You OK?" she asked. "After our talk this afternoon I just thought you might be down in the dumps."

"I am, but I'll get over it. I always do."

"Want to come over for a glass of wine or some coffee or something? Charlie went down early so I've got some time to myself this evening."

"That's nice of you but you don't need to feel sorry for me. I told you because you needed to know, not because I was looking for some sympathy."

"How could I not sympathize, though? That's my nature, why I became a pediatrician. I have great sympathy for children. Kids are great. They don't complain, they're brave, they do what they need to do without making a fuss over it. I fell in love with the field my first day in and that was that."

"Pretty much the same with me. I intended to be an anesthesiologist but this is what worked out for me and I'm glad it did. Kids are fun to treat most of the time. After my divorce and before I came to Lakeside Clinic I was doubting my choice a little, thinking maybe I should go back and become a pediatric anesthesiologist or specialist in something like pediatric oncology. Something to change my life. But that was all because I'd lost Amy and she was like my compass in a lot of ways. Then I came here and realized I'm where I belong. No turning back. No changing."

"Well, it's never too late to change, if you're thinking about it. Nothing wrong with shaking things up."

He chuckled. "I think I've got a little too much water under my bridge to change my field at this stage of the game. Besides, I like what I do. General care is good. It's what I want to do because I like the interactions as well as the dynamics of the whole field. And in a day and age when so many people are specializing, or where so many family-care practitioners are seeing children, I think the place of the general-practice pediatrician is more needed than ever. Besides, kids are fun."

"Give it some thought, though, since it's still obviously on your mind. Lakeside has a good anesthesiology program. Then there are other hospitals with equally good reputations, as well."

"I've given it a lot of thought, but I'm where I want to be. Either in a clinic or in the ER."

"Well, you're good at what you do, and if you're

happy there..." She quieted for a minute, then said, "Could you hang on for a second? I hear Charlie crying, and I'm not sure he's feeling so well this evening. I'll be back on in a minute."

"How about I let you go and I'll see you tomorrow?" he responded. "Charlie could take a little while, and I don't want to rush you."

"Tomorrow," she said, then hung up, smiling. It was nice having Simon for a friend. Although it did make her wish she had room in her life for something more.

For the first time in her motherhood experience, except for one brief exception, Charlie slept all the way through the night, which should have elated Del but actually it bothered her. He was restless, kept himself curled into a ball with his little legs drawn up to his chest, and didn't get the restful sleep she'd hoped he would. Then when by morning he was still fussy she knew he definitely wasn't feeling good. But another preliminary check showed him to be in good shape. No cough, no runny nose, no fever. Just grouchy again, and he definitely didn't want to be held, which was unusual. He also refused to eat. In fact, he threw his bowl of oatmeal on the floor, which was, perhaps, the most alarming thing of all as Charlie had a pretty hefty morning appetite and loved his oatmeal and bananas. So rather than taking him to day care first thing, she took him to the clinic to get an unbiased opinion of what could possibly be wrong since she had a suspicion she knew and it was best not to treat him herself. Not that she could, if she was right about this.

"Simon," she said on the way in, "would you mind looking at Charlie for me and seeing what you can come up with? He started acting fussy last night and, while I have my suspicions, I'd rather not be the one diagnosing him."

"Take him to Room One and I'll be right there," he said as he slung on his white lab coat and followed her into the exam room. "So what are his symptoms?" he asked, listening first to his chest, then his tummy.

"Fussy, won't eat, doesn't want to be held and he balls up in a fetal position when I put him down. He was fine last night. Slept all night, was a little fussy when I put him down but he didn't display any overt symptoms."

"Knees drawn up to his chest?" Simon asked.

Del nodded.

"Has he ever had an intussusception?" This was a condition where intestine folded into another section of intestine, much like the way a collapsing telescope folded up into the section in front of it. In and of itself the condition was not serious in the first couple days but it did carry with it a risk of surgery if not treated soon enough. Especially if an intestinal blockage occurred.

Del sighed out loud and her hands started to shake. "No. Did we catch it in time or will he need surgery?"

"If his symptoms just came on him last night or this morning, he's probably a good candidate for treatment without surgery."

Del brushed back a tear. "I didn't miss it, did I?"

Simon shook his head. "You brought him in as soon as he presented with symptoms. Don't second-guess yourself, Del. Babies have no way of telling us what's wrong and if he's not showing symptoms, you can't just guess there's something wrong or you'd drive yourself crazy. You were observant and you did the right thing as quickly as you knew."

She brushed back another tear. "It's so difficult sometimes. So many things could go wrong."

"And so many things could go right."

"I guess so, but when it's your child…" She shrugged.

"You're a normal mom, doctor or not. And most moms would be scared by the diagnosis."

"So how are you going to treat him?"

"Conservatively at first. I'd like to start with an ultrasound followed by an abdominal X-ray just to make sure that the bowel hasn't gone necrotic. And we'll go from there. But he does need to be hospitalized for the procedures and to be watched for a day or two. You do understand that, don't you?"

She nodded. "He's going to be so frightened."

"He may surprise you. One of the reasons I like kids so much is that they take things better than we do. If someone told me my intestine was twisted up I'd be in a panic, but Charlie will just accept things as they come his way."

"He will, won't he?" she said, trying to muster up some conviction in her voice even though she was scared to death.

"Look, Del. You've seen this before and treated it. It's usually not a complicated procedure once the diagnosis is confirmed." He prodded Charlie's belly for a mass and sure enough, there it was. "You know the outcome is good in most of these cases. And if he does need to have surgery, it's a relatively simple procedure."

"I've treated it, but never in my child. He's always been so healthy."

"And he still is healthy," Simon reassured her. He was thinking back to when Amy was sent home from school with the measles. He'd been on call and hadn't seen much of her for a couple of days, then to see his daughter all covered with a rash the way she was—at first he'd been angry that her mother had allowed her to go to school that way, then he'd turned his concern to Amy, who had been one mighty sick little girl for a few days. He'd felt so helpless and vulnerable because there really had been nothing to do for her except sit with Amy and help her ride out the illness. Because of that, he knew how Del was feeling and his heart went out to her because she, too, was feeling so helpless and vulnerable right now. And blaming herself.

"So here's what I propose," he said to Del. "First we get him admitted to the hospital and get the diagnosis over with, then we discuss the options. And even though you know, it falls down this way. He'll be treated with either a barium or water-soluble contrast enema or an air-contrast enema, which will confirm the intussusception, and in the best possible scenario reduce it. The success rate is pretty good—about eighty percent. If this does recur, it should happen in about twenty-four hours, and that's when a surgeon will open the abdomen and manually squeeze the part that has telescoped. Or the surgeon may choose to reduce the problem by laparoscopy. Any way you go, it's going to be more stressful on you than it will be on Charlie. Best case scenario puts him in the eighty percent category and he'll be home in a couple of days. Worst case is surgery, which means he'll be here a little longer than that."

"I appreciate you going over this with me. Of course I know it, but right now I'd be hard pressed to tell you my name let alone anything else."

"It's Del," he said, smiling.

She smiled. "Will you be there during the tests and/or surgery?"

"If they let me. And if you request it."

"I'll request it," she said, "because I don't want him to be alone, and I know they won't let me anywhere near him while they're doing whatever it is they've got to do." She looked at her little boy lying there on the exam table all drawn up in a ball, then bent and kissed him. "I'm trusting you with my son, Simon. He's the best thing in my life and I'm handing his care over to you."

Simon swallowed hard. He knew what it was like to surrender your child. "I'll take good care of him, like he's my own."

"I'm counting on that," Del said as she reached out and took hold of Simon's hand and held on for dear life. "I'm really counting on that."

CHAPTER SEVEN

THE PROCEDURE TOOK longer than she expected and it was nice having Simon sit there with her, holding her hand at first, then holding on to her when her nerves finally got the best of her and her whole body started shaking. “It’s so much worse when it’s your child,” she said, fighting back tears of fear and anguish. “Even though I know he’s getting good care.”

He ran his thumb over the back of her soft hand. “He’ll be fine,” Simon reassured her, even though she didn’t feel much as if reassurances were going to work.

“Sure. But still, suppose this doesn’t work and he has to move on to the next step, which is surgery?” She grabbed hold of his hand and clung tightly to him. “I don’t know if I could get through it, the thought of them having to remove a piece of his intestine. That’s so serious. And the risks so great it scares me to death. I mean, what if…?”

He stroked her cheek. “One thing at a time, Del. That’s what I always tell the parents of my patients. We’ll deal with one thing at a time, get through it and hope for the best. That’s all you can do.”

She exhaled a big, wobbly breath. "Easy to say when the shoe is on the other foot. But when it's on your own..." She shut her eyes as the tears streamed down her cheeks. "When it's your own child it's different. He's my flesh and blood, Simon, and he's suffering. But there's nothing I can do to fix this. I'm the mother. I should be taking care of him."

"You can't just center your entire life around what he wants or needs. You need to have something in there for you, too, and that's your medical practice, no matter how hard it is to be a single parent as well as a full-time doctor. It's called balancing your life."

"But how did you do it?"

"It wasn't easy, and I'll be the first one to admit that. Amy came first, but my medical practice had its place in there, as well. I learned to balance it so we were both happy."

"How?"

"First, by realizing that I was happier having a life in medicine than I was without it. When I was happier, Amy was happier. I think by balancing myself I evened out everything for the both of us, which was difficult because the older she got, the more she recognized that her mother simply didn't care enough to be involved. Which made for some awfully moody moments. Except, she always had me and she counted on that. I just had to make sure I never missed out on the important things going on in her life. That was the tricky part, too, I'll admit. Amy needed me, my practice needed me and for a while even Yvette needed me. I suppose you can say I failed Yvette, but I think she set up the situation between us to fail." He shrugged. "There was nothing I could do about that, but I did have control over the rest of it, no matter how difficult it became. I just had to make sure that Amy never missed out because of anything else going on in my life."

"I admire that in you, Simon. I'm not sure my priorities are that clear yet. For me it's all Charlie and nothing else. Even my medical practice takes a backseat, which I know it shouldn't. But Charlie is so important to me that I'd love to retire and stay home with him. And I might for a while except I know I'd miss my practice and wouldn't be completely happy not working. It's a real dilemma."

"There were days I certainly hated walking away from Amy, so I understand."

"But you figured it out."

"After a while."

"When I had Charlie I was fiercely adamant that I could have it all, and I didn't count on the emotional turmoil I'm facing now. But there are days when I hand him over to day care that I'm literally so conflicted I don't know what to do."

"You do the best you can. That's all that can be expected from any of us. And the thing is, you can have it all. You already do...at least all that you want."

"What would I do if I did get involved with someone? Maybe even got married? There's not enough of me to go around. I couldn't do it."

"Sure you could, if that's what you wanted. You'd just have to marry the right person. The one who understands that you have this huge life going on already.

He'd certainly have to be patient. You'd choose wisely." He smiled. "Because you've had what you know you don't want, I'm willing to bet you've put some thinking into what you do want."

The surgery ward door pushed open and Del's heart doubled its rhythm, but it wasn't for her. Nothing to do with Charlie, but some other surgery waiters got a bit of good news judging from the round of cheers that went up.

After the noise of the happy waiters died down, she continued, "I've never really given it that much thought because I'm not sure anybody would want to handle my life, such as it is. It's so full already that I don't think I'd have room to add anything or anyone else. And I don't want to get involved when those are my expectations."

"But you could be missing out."

"Or not," she responded. "I mean, look at everything I've got. That's enough to keep me busy."

"But don't you get lonely when you go to bed alone every night?"

"Don't you?" she countered.

"I'd be lying if I said I didn't. But I've got different standards this time. And I'm going to be very careful if I get involved again."

"Let me guess. No women with children."

He arched his eyebrows. "I'm not opposed to children. In fact, I'd love to have a large family. But I don't want to be put in a position where the kids can be taken away from me. Next time I'm a dad, I want to be a dad for real."

"Poor child," Del said. "To count on someone so much then have him kicked out of her life."

Simon shrugged. "And not to know what she's doing. Sometimes I feel...lost.'

"But Amy lost, too, didn't she?"

"I hope not, but I can't help but think that she did. It keeps me up at nights sometimes wondering and worrying."

"I wouldn't do that to Charlie, which is why I'm happy just the way things are. But today...it's not what I bargained for, and that's stupid of me, considering how I'm a pediatrician. I mean, I know better. Kids get sick with all kinds of strange ailments and I guess I always thought I'd be exempt since I'm a professional in the field. But it doesn't work that way, does it?"

"Amy broke her arm once. She fell down a flight of stairs and the break was pretty substantial. Her mother was out of town, so that left me alone to deal with it and I don't know when I've ever felt more helpless than I did when she was getting it casted. But she came through it better than I did, just the way Charlie will come through this better than you do. I promise."

"Amy needs you as her father. Her mother did a really stupid thing taking her away from you."

"I agree with you on that. I would have done anything for that little girl." He shook his head. "Which is the reason I won't date another woman with a child because, if something should come of it, I stand a very good chance of having that child yanked away from me after I've formed an attachment."

"I can't blame you. If someone came and took Charlie away from me…" She brushed back a straying tear. "Just call me an overprotective mother. I know I am, and I'll admit it."

"Nothing wrong with that. Better to be overprotective than to be Amy's mother, who looks at her daughter as an inconvenience."

"Well, Charlie's not an inconvenience!" Del sniffed. "And I'd fight anybody who said he was."

Simon laughed. He liked that attitude of a mother lion, wished he'd seen it more in his own home with Amy. But Yvette had never cared that much and she was always glad to give up the chore of child care to someone else so she could have her life to herself. Honestly, had he seen that in her when they were married, they wouldn't have been married. But he'd been blinded by a great body and good looks, and back then he'd been too young to look any further. Now he knew, and he was on his guard against the type.

The thing was, Del could have been his type, as fierce as she was, but he wasn't about to put himself into that position again.

"You're a good mother," he told Del.

"With a sick son. I'm so worried, Simon. I know there was nothing I could do but it's still so easy to kick myself about it."

"If this is the worst he ever goes through you'll be one lucky lady. Kids get sick every day. If they didn't we'd have to find a new line of work."

She chuckled. "You're so good to me, Simon. You know exactly what to say and when to say it."

"Comes from practice. Years and years of practice.

Just doing my job," he said, letting up a little on his grip around her for fear he was cutting off her circulation. Either that or creating a dependence he could ill afford to develop.

"This is going above and beyond the call," she replied, snuggling back into him. "And I appreciate it."

He knew he should pull away from her right now, but he liked the feel of her pressed tight to him, and it wouldn't take much for him to ask her out on a rightful date when this crisis was over. Of course, he wouldn't. She was a single mom and he'd promised himself he wouldn't do that. So as much as he liked Del, even cared for her, he wasn't going back on his word. Friendship was as far as he was taking it. Although, he wasn't quite ready to define the level of that friendship yet.

Another snuggle and he'd be lost, he was sure. Yet he didn't have it in him to pull back from her, especially not now when she needed him so badly. So he tightened up a bit, braced his back as well as his resolve and endured the feeling passing through him, the one that told him it would be very easy to develop feelings for Del. Whether or not they'd turn out to be serious feelings, he didn't know, but there was some kind of feelings there nonetheless.

They sat there together like that for the next hour, with her clinging and him regretting until the pediatrician on call came out and told them that Charlie's barium enema seemed to have worked out the kink just fine.

"I want to keep him here for a couple days to watch

him," Dr. Knowles said. "But right now everything looks good."

"He's sleeping?" Del asked, pulling away from Simon and adjusting her white lab coat.

"Sound asleep, and I'd like to keep him that way for a few hours, if we can, so when you go in to see him try and be quiet."

Del nodded. Then looked at Simon, who'd backed away from the whole scene. "You coming with me?" she asked him.

"No, I don't think so. The more of us in the room, the more likely the odds of disturbing him are. So I think I'll go back over to the clinic for now and catch up with you later on."

"I'm grateful for your support, Simon," she said, reaching out to take his hand. It was soft and gentle and large the way he was. "I couldn't have gotten through this on my own."

"Call me if you need anything," Simon said, then nodded to Dr. Knowles. "Thank you for what you did to help Charlie," he said, then turned and left the waiting area.

Brian Knowles smiled. "You make a cute family," he said.

"We're not a family. Simon's just a friend."

"Couldn't tell that from where I was watching."

"Then you were watching from the wrong spot because Simon and I have nothing going between us." Even though she wanted to, her feelings were growing so strong for him.

"Well, I've seen families with a whole lot less going

on between them. All I can say is, you look good together, and Simon looks like he really cares."

There was no point in arguing the matter with the pediatrician. He'd already made up his mind and had her and Simon and Charlie posed together as a family. Of course, maybe that was what it looked like, the way she'd clung to Simon during the entire procedure. "When can I see him?" Del asked.

"Now. He's in Recovery, but you can go sit with him there, then after he's transferred to a regular room you can spend as much time with him as you want."

"Was there anything I could have done?" she asked nervously.

"Just what you did. It's a relatively rare condition and one that doesn't always get caught in time. I'd say, between you and Simon, you did an excellent job of catching and diagnosing it before it progressed too far. As for whether or not it's cured, time will tell, but I'm willing to bet it's probably a one-time incident. At least I hope it is." Dr. Knowles shook hands with Del and exited the room, leaving her standing there alone, feeling grateful and scared all at the same time. She didn't want to be alone just yet, but Simon had made it abundantly clear his involvement there was done. She was glad for as much of him as she'd gotten, but she wanted more just now. Wanted his comfort again, as she was still upset and his seemed to be the calming influence that had got her through.

It was three hours before Charlie was moved into a private room, and Del was right there with him every step of the way. Simon had called once, albeit a very brief and businesslike call. And Dr. Knowles had stepped in to have a look one time, pleased with the results so far. "It's looking good," he said to Del, as he hurried back out to see another patient. Leaving her and Charlie there virtually alone again, except for an occasional check by a nurse.

"You scared me to death," she told her son as she took hold of his hand and he gripped on for dear life. "But you're going to be fine. The doctor said you're making a good recovery so far."

"I understand you've arranged for more time off work," Simon said from the doorway. "I was going to put in the request for you, but you beat me to it."

"That's what I said I was going to do." She shrugged, secretly glad to see him, and trying to act aloof about her feelings all at the same time. "I'm used to doing things on my own."

"Well, I wasn't sure if that was you or a panic attack talking." He smiled as he walked over to the crib and looked down on Charlie. "Good-looking boy," he said. "He looks just like you."

She smiled. "I'm surprised you came back. I thought maybe I'd scared you off earlier, being so clingy."

"Your son was having a procedure. You were entitled to be clingy. So, what's the word?"

"So far it's all good. He can go home day after tomorrow if everything goes well."

"It will," Simon said confidently. "And in the meantime, I've ordered a pizza to be sent here to the hospital since I figured you haven't eaten all day."

"I hadn't," she admitted. "Too worried."

"Well, I ordered large because I thought I'd hang around and split it with you, if you don't mind."

"I'd welcome the company. And the pizza," she added, realizing how hungry she was now that the ordeal was over.

Dinner was neither fancy nor romantic, but she appreciated the gesture. In fact, had he not reminded her she hadn't eaten at all, she probably would have gone the rest of the day and maybe had some graham crackers from the nurses' station. But Simon had been so kind and thoughtful that she wondered why he was still single. Not every woman out there had a child and certainly he could have and probably should have attracted someone who liked him for all his endearing qualities. Maybe he just wasn't ready. Or he was mistrustful, which was certainly something she understood.

"This was awfully nice of you," she said, debating her second slice of pizza. "Does your ex-wife know what she let get away?"

"More like shoved out the door. She was all set for wealthy and I wasn't."

"Doctors aren't always wealthy," Del defended. "I'm comfortable, but you could hardly consider it wealthy."

"A lot of people don't understand that. Especially my ex. I had student loans to pay back, a family to support. It was a lot of responsibility."

"A lot of people don't count, but your ex should have in the manner in which she expected things from you. Personally, I'm not all that concerned with the material gains in my life. I want to make Charlie comfortable but I don't need to be wealthy to do that."

"So if the man you decided on was temporarily tapped out..."

"Wouldn't matter one way or another. I'm looking for character and integrity. Someone who'll be decent to my son and grow to love him. That's more important than anything else, at least in my opinion." Someone like Simon, she thought to herself. He would be the perfect man in her life, if he wanted to get involved. Of course, he didn't, which made her wary of her growing feelings for him.

"So would you ever find yourself in a relationship with someone who wasn't so tapped out as you are?"

"Depends on who she is, I suppose. My next go around, if there ever is another one, is going to be with someone who's down to earth, someone who values things other than financial gain."

"And her financial status wouldn't matter to you?"

He shrugged. "Get me to that point and we'll see. I'd like to think I'm more responsible than that but who knows? We all make our mistakes, I guess. Mine was thinking she'd change."

Del laughed. "That's what I thought, too. You know, you wake up one morning with the person you want who has magically changed overnight from the person you had."

"I stayed for Amy's sake and look where that got me." He sighed as he closed the pizza box. "None of it's predictable."

"Is that why you haven't gotten together with someone else?"

"Big mistrust factors on my part, and I'll admit it," Simon said. "I proved what kind of a bad choice I made the first time and I don't want to go there again. So for me it's easier being single."

"I get the mistrust factor. That's why I had Charlie with no one else involved. I wanted a baby but I didn't want someone else involved who might injure him the way I was injured during my relationship with Eric. Bringing up a baby alone was my choice and a good option for someone my age, I think."

"But don't you ever wish you had someone there to share parenting duties with? Another person who loves him as much as you do, who can help you when you need it?"

"I never thought I did, until today. But today was out of the ordinary."

"So what happens next time he gets sick and there's no one around to help you? I can tell you from experience it's easier raising a child with two parents than one. That's the kind of built-in support you need."

"But from the way you tell it, you had only you."

"I did. Yvette was more than happy to pass Amy off on me and it wasn't easy working and raising a child all at the same time. I really wanted things to be different, where she assumed part of the parenting chore, but she never did. I was the designated parent in the relationship and she was the one who was free and clear to do what she wanted without the involvement. In fact, if she hadn't met someone else I have an idea she would have still hung onto me because she knew how deep my feelings for Amy were."

"And you would have stayed?"

"Probably."

Del shook her head. "Sounds to me like I'm better off being a single parent than having someone else around who doesn't care as much as I do."

"The thing is, parenting is a tough job and the older they get, the tougher it gets. Charlie's just a baby right now, but what about when he's five or six and needs a man around?"

"What about when he's five or six and doesn't need a man around?" she asked him. "Not all kids have two parents and most of them turn out just fine."

"But how do the parents turn out? What happens when you don't have someone to lean on?"

"Then I don't lean. It's as simple as that."

"You needed me today, Del."

"Because I was scared and this was Charlie's first real sickness outside a cold. And it wasn't about Charlie anyway. It was about my weakness. But I'll get better as I get more used to being a single mother."

"Maybe you will. Personally, though, I never got over needing someone else to help me raise Amy, and she had a mother."

"We all make our choices, Simon. You chose to raise Amy the way you did and I chose to have Charlie and raise him the way I am. Initially, I didn't get any support from my parents. They thought it was crazy. But once they saw their grandson…" She shrugged. "They changed, I changed and everything in my life changed all because of my decision. If you'd been allowed to stay and raise Amy your life would have been different, too."

"Which is why I won't do that again. It rips your heart out when the child isn't yours and you've got no legal claim."

"So we've both exercised alternately good and poor judgment that got us where we are today. What can I say?"

"That we're human." He stood and picked up the pizza box. "Look, I've got to go. I'll be working for two for a couple of weeks and I need to get to bed early tonight. If you need anything, give me a call...I assume you're spending the night here."

"I am. And thanks, but I'll be fine."

"Need some clean clothes? I can drop them by in the morning?"

"I was thinking about running home once Charlie's down for the night, grabbing a shower and changing my clothes, then coming back here and sleeping." She pointed to the bed next to the crib. "Not comfortable, but it will do in a pinch."

"How about breakfast in the morning? Or coffee?"

"Coffee would be lovely, but you really don't have to take care of me, Simon. I'm good on my own."

"Which is why you hadn't eaten today?"

She smiled up at him. "It would have come up at some point. I'm not a martyr to the cause."

"I think you are, but that's an opinion we'll save for another day since I really do need to get home."

"Thanks for everything you've done today."

"My pleasure," he said, thinking it was his guilty

pleasure as he enjoyed his time with Del way more than he intended to.

"I'll…I'll see you around. Maybe I'll stop in the clinic when I know Charlie's one hundred percent."

"Or maybe I'll stop by your place one night and bring dinner. There's this great Chinese restaurant just down the street from me and…"

"Ming's?" she asked as her eyes lit up.

"Ming's," he answered. "Great—"

"Egg rolls!" she finished his sentence. "I like the vegetarian."

"And I like the pork."

"So we have a difference of opinion," she said, laughing as Charlie started to cry. He was strapped down with so many tubes and monitors it looked uncomfortable to her so she knew it had to be to him. She stood from her chair and picked him up gently so as not to disturb his IV or his NG tube.

"And on that note I'll say good-night and leave you two alone."

She'd gone home, taken her shower, changed her clothes and packed an overnight bag for both her and Charlie and headed right back to the hospital only to find him still sound asleep. It had been quite the ordeal for him today, and one for her, as well. Without Simon…well, she didn't even want to think how her day would have progressed without him. Going through all that alone just wasn't appealing. She had called her parents, who were on their way back from Costa Rica to help out, which she appreciated, but that help was a little too late, and for the first time ever Simon, combined with Charlie's illness, had showed her just how utterly alone she was as a parent.

It had never scared her before but now it unsettled her knowing she was in this all by herself without a nearby shoulder to cry on. Truth was, she didn't have a lot of friends—her job had taken care of that. And she had no brothers or sisters. Not even any cousins she could call on. So her backup plan was, well…no one. Which was why she was so glad to have Simon there with her for support. Not that she considered him her backup plan or anything like that. In fact, she wasn't even sure she considered him more than a casual friend yet. But things seemed to be leaning in a different direction, which made her glad he wasn't interested in anything more than a casual friendship because that would signal the end of things between them, since casual was all she wanted. Two peas in a pod, she decided. They both wanted the same thing for different reasons. How absurd was that?

He probably shouldn't have been so forthright with her about the way she was bringing up Charlie, as it was none of his business how she raised her child, whether that be alone or with someone else to help her. But he remembered how difficult it had been raising Amy without any help and the older she'd got, the more help he'd needed. It hadn't been easy, being a daddy without much of a clue, but he wouldn't have changed a moment of it because he'd loved that little girl. Still did. And he'd take her back in a heartbeat if her mother ever cared to give her up, which wasn't going to happen as Amy was a shining star who drew other people in. Yvette used that to her advantage. Took every chance she could to push Amy right on out there.

So he'd wanted to impart his wisdom, except his situation with Amy was nothing like Del's with Charlie. She'd made her choice and the one thing he knew for sure was that Del would never use Charlie as a pawn in her own schemes the way Yvette did with Amy. Del's love for her baby was true all the way.

Still, he didn't want to see things going so hard on Del and he knew they were right now, judging from the way she'd clung so desperately to him yesterday. It was as if he were the starch she needed to keep herself from collapsing, and if something ever happened to Charlie when he wasn't there to hold on to Del, he wondered how she'd manage to get through it. Her true colors as a caring mother had really shown through, but so had her frailties over being alone. Except, she wouldn't admit that was what he'd been seeing. One good, objective look was all it took, though. From him, even from her if she weren't so personally involved.

Admittedly, though, he'd liked being important for her in that time. Liked the way she'd held on to him, the feel of her hands grasping him, the way she wouldn't let go. It was nice being needed. Maybe even a little wanted. Especially by Del. But who was he kidding? It was a one-time event, born out of her need for comfort. That was all it had been, all it could be. After all, she had a child and he refused to put himself through that again. Once was too much. Probably for her, too, once she'd had time to think about it.

Simon sighed as he went to Exam Four to check out a youngster with type one diabetes. Both parents were there, both were equally concerned, even though they were newly divorced. That was the way a child should be raised, he thought as he knocked on the door then entered the room. Yes, that was definitely the way a child should be raised. Only he'd missed his chance and Del didn't want hers.

Weren't they the perfectly mismatched couple? he thought as he flipped on the computer screen in the room and took a look at the child's blood work. "Good job," he said to the little girl, who was about Amy's age. "Everything's in perfect order and it's all looking the way it should."

Everything but his life. And maybe a little bit of Del's life, as well.

CHAPTER EIGHT

It was a week from the day of Charlie's successful procedure to the day when Del showed up at work. "Only a week off?" Simon asked her on his way in to examine a bug bite in Exam Three.

"My parents want some quality time with their grandson and that doesn't include me, I'm afraid. Besides, they're both retired doctors so who better to watch him for a few hours?"

"I talked to your dad on the phone the other night, when I was thinking about bringing dinner by. He's awfully protective of you. And of his grandson, too."

"So that's why you never came over?"

"They'd already eaten by the time I called. He seemed like a nice man, though. Reminded me a lot of you… straightforward, honest, overprotective of his child."

Del laughed out loud. "That's what a protective parent does. He watches after his kid even when his kid is thirty-five years old."

"And that will be you and Charlie in another few years. You won't exactly warn off the girls he'll want to date but you won't be overly friendly, either."

"Like father, like daughter, I suppose."

"Anyway, I'm glad you came back early. We're short staffed, as you already know. Dr. Kent went into early labor and Dr. Morgan is off with the flu. So we're really down on our numbers and we could use the help."

"Which is why I came in today. I'd intended to stay home with Charlie and my parents another week, but the clinic needs me even more than Charlie does since he adores his grandparents, so I was feeling a bit useless." She shrugged. "Meaning I'm back."

"How's Charlie?"

"Doing nicely. No flare-ups, no real disruption to his routine unless you could call grandparents a disruption. He had his incident and it was cured, and, even though the doctor wants to follow him for a couple of months, there don't seem to be any bad consequences."

"Good to hear that. Look, the board's full, and, even though you're one of the bosses and owners of the clinic, all I can do is tell you to take your pick of patients. We're busy today."

"And I was so looking forward to Ming's egg rolls," she teased as she took the first chart off the top of the stack then logged it into the computer. "At least now I know why you didn't bring them. My daddy scared you off." She almost strangled herself she laughed so hard.

"He didn't scare me. He just made it abundantly clear that my attention wasn't wanted or needed."

She reached up and ran her hand over his cheek. "I needed your attention."

"Well, just name the time and place and you've got it."

"Ming's tonight, after work. My parents won't mind. In fact, I think they'll be glad to have extra time alone with Charlie. They don't get much time with him and it will be good for all of them."

"Allows them their time," he said. "Makes for good luck all the way around. That's what your fortune cookie will tell you."

It was sometime midafternoon, after Charlie's lunch, when Simon caught up to Del. "You look like you could use a cup of coffee or tea," he told her.

"I lost a patient today," Del said. "Not as in dying but as in yanking her kid out of the clinic, and it drained me. And I got pretty indignant with the girl's mother. Child's anorexic and the mom was pretty disgusted with the girl and I, in turn, got pretty disgusted with the girl's mom. And of course I couldn't say anything."

"For what it's worth, I think your indignation toward that girl's mother was righteous in every way. I know what it's like to deal with a parent who thinks it's all about them."

"Amy's mother," she murmured.

He nodded. "Trust me, there were plenty of times when I had a whole string of things I wanted to say to Yvette, but didn't because it wasn't in Amy's best interest."

"Is there a day that goes by when you don't think about her?"

"Not a day. Some days it's worse than others, though."

"I'm so sorry."

"Me, too. And thanks."

* * *

As the rest of the day pressed on, things settled down into a normal routine. Del saw a few regular patients, helped with the overflow, and nothing was out of the ordinary. Not the ailments, not even the minor emergencies. It was the kind of day everyone wanted and drove you crazy when you got it. But as the day progressed, she found herself looking forward to her dinner date at Ming's, and it wasn't the egg rolls that were stirring her. Del was actually excited about her date with Simon. Just the two of them in a quaint little hole in the wall. It had all the earmarks of being romantic, even though romance wasn't what she wanted from him. But she did like his company, loved his conversation, enjoyed their alone time together. It was amazing how in just a few weeks he'd become so important to her. And dinner at Ming's was just the icing on the cake as far as she was concerned.

Was there potential in their relationship? Possibly? Maybe even probably. Except he'd made it pretty darned clear he wasn't interested in getting involved with a woman who had a child. Who could blame him for that? Certainly, she couldn't, after the way his last relationship had turned out. Couldn't they have a casual fling though? One without commitments? One that could even be platonic if that was what he wanted in order to keep himself safe. Certainly, she wanted that safety net, too, and she'd made up her mind not to get so deeply involved that intense emotions came into play.

They took a seat by the front window, where they could look out over the lake, and if there ever was something that called for romance, this was it. The restaurant itself was tiny and intimate and the decor was like stepping back into old-world China, where a jade Buddha sat on a shelf, and beaded curtains separated the front from the back room. The room was bathed in reds and black and the smells coming from the kitchen were enough to make her mouth water the instant Simon opened the front door and she heard the quaint, old-fashioned doorbell jingle on entry.

And the lake… Del loved the vastness of it. Ming's sat on the other side of the busy Lakeshore Drive, opposite the lake, but because the lake itself there was so beautiful she didn't even notice the traffic up and down that stretch of road in front of it. All she could see was the sun setting over the water, casting it in the glow of golds and navy blues. And all she could hear was the faint strain of Chinese music playing in the background.

"I haven't actually been in here since, well, it was a long time before Charlie was born. This place always seemed like it was for couples and being a single in an establishment for two just didn't feel right. So I ordered takeout, or had it delivered. Made it less pathetic that way, I think."

"You think of being single as pathetic?" he asked her as he took the menus from the server's hand.

"In a restaurant that caters to romance, yes. In my normal day-to-day life, no."

"I've come in here alone before and eaten."

"Then you're braver than I am, Simon, or at least less self-conscious."

"But you've got nothing to feel self-conscious about.

You made your choice and you don't regret it, so that should include dining out even if it is a romantic restaurant. Especially if you like the food."

"I love the food here. It's the best Chinese I've ever had. Everything prepared to order.'

"Like your life, where everything's prepared to order."

"And what's so different about your life?" she asked.

"I venture out of my comfort zone for one thing. I don't think you do."

"Maybe not so much, but I have Charlie to consider."

"And you couldn't bring him here with you?"

"Maybe when he's older." She looked up at the server, who was patiently awaiting drink orders. "I'll have unsweet iced tea," she said. "With a lot of lemon."

"And I'll have a beer. Whatever you have on tap is fine. And could you bring us a couple of egg rolls as appetizers, one pork and one vegetarian?"

The girl scrambled away to fetch the orders while Del and Simon continued talking. "I think the ambiance here would be lost on Charlie, anyway."

"But not on you, and you do count in the mother-son relationship. You can build your life around him to the point that you're suffocating him and I don't think that's your intent, is it?"

"Charlie goes out with me."

"Where?"

"To the park, and the grocery store. Sometimes we just go for a walk. He likes that."

"But where do you go for yourself?"

"Same places Charlie goes," she said, reaching

across the table for a packet of sweetener. He laid his hand atop hers for a moment. “How long has it been since you’ve been on a real date?”

She thought a minute. “It’s been about eight years. I got tangled up with Eric for five, then I was recovering from that, then I got pregnant and next thing you know I had Charlie.”

“Eight years? How could you deprive yourself for so long?”

“You were married, Simon. How long has it been for you?”

He winced. “About the same.”

“So we’re alike in that.” She took the tea the server brought to the table and dumped the packet of sweetener in it while Simon took a swig of his beer, then sighed.

“We are alike in some ways, aren’t we?”

“More than I like to think about,” she said, pushing out her plate to take her oversized egg roll.

“So this is both our first dates in years.”

“Except we’re not dating,” Del reminded him.

“Just having dinner for two in a romantic little hideaway. Sounds like a date to me.”

Del shook her head as she cut off a bite of her egg roll and dipped it in sweet-and-sour sauce. “I accepted dinner, pure and simple. I wouldn’t have accepted if you’d asked me out on a date. In fact, I’m fully prepared to pay for my own dinner, which makes this even more of a non-date.”

“So I’m on a date and you’re not. I suppose we could leave it at that.”

"But I thought you didn't want to get involved with a woman with children."

"A date doesn't always mean an involvement. Sometimes a date's just a date and nothing more. Or less." He ate a large bite of his egg roll then picked up his menu. "So, do you want to order separately, or do you want to do the dinner for two, which starts with egg drop soup and goes from there?"

"They do have awfully good egg drop soup," she commented. "So if you want to go with the dinner for two..." She shrugged. "Why not? That could be my concession to our non-date date."

Simon chuckled. "You're stubborn. Did anybody ever tell you that before?"

"I wasn't for a lot of years. But when I broke clear of Eric that was one of the first things I worked on. I was in counseling and the doctor told me I had a lot of work to do on me and finding myself again. Which I did."

"You still in counseling, or is that too personal to ask?"

"Nope, not in counseling. I graduated from that when I decided I wanted a baby."

"How did that come up?"

"It didn't just come up. I've always wanted a baby and I thought—stupidly—Eric was the one. By the time I knew he wasn't I was in too deep. But that desire in me never changed. I still wanted a baby, just not his. So I jumped at the chance after we broke up. Actually, not jumped so much as gave it some long, hard thinking before I knew I could do it. And what about you and Amy?"

"I didn't know she was part of the picture when I married Yvette. Amy was never mentioned and at the time her father had custody. But he didn't want her so after we were married about six months there she was on the doorstep one day. A man with a toddler with a little suitcase of clothes, telling Yvette he was finished with the father things. Honest to God, that was the first time I knew of her existence and we'd been married for nearly six months. I suppose that's why I could never pin her down on having a family—she already had one she didn't want."

"That's rough."

"It was. But I think I grew into being a pretty good dad. Problem was, Yvette wanted someone more exciting than a dad, but Amy needed a parent." He sighed. "And life goes on."

"But you got hurt in the deal."

"Not as much as Amy did. That last day when I finally had to say goodbye she clung to me, crying, begging not to be taken from me." He sniffed. "I've never felt so helpless in all my life."

Their soup arrived before anything else could be said, followed by their chow mein, followed by deep-fried bananas and by the time they reached their fortune cookies, Del was almost too full to have the strength to open hers up. But she did.

You will have a lucky night.

Simon's said: *This will be a night to remember.*

"I think they have two different boxes of cookies—

one with regular fortunes, and ones they give to the couple they believe will find romance." Del wadded up her fortune and tossed it on the table. "So much for that," she said, taking a bite of the cookie, then leaving the rest on her plate. "The only luck I'm going to have tonight is if I didn't gain five pounds eating so much good food."

"Well, mine's coming true as we speak because this is definitely a night to remember."

"But for how long? And for what reason?"

"Probably until I get senile, and the reason...I'm enjoying the company of my first date in all these years."

"Married years don't count?"

"Says who?"

"Says me," Del replied, looking at her crumpled fortune. "And that's all that counts."

"Whoa. You're the only one who's entitled to an opinion?"

She nodded. "In my life I am."

"But this is my life, too."

"And you're entitled to your opinion, however wrong it may be."

"Spoken like someone who was in a marriage-like situation for five years."

"Close to marriage, but not marriage. So it doesn't count. And for what it's worth, after we became a couple he never *dated* me again." She took out her credit card to pay her portion of the bill and Simon rejected it. "You can pick up the whole tab next time."

"It's a deal," she said, realizing suddenly that he'd

taken the advantage here by getting her to commit to a second date. "If there is another time."

He arched wickedly provocative eyebrows. "There'll be a second time, if for no other reason than you owe me a dinner out."

"Aren't you the tricky one?" she said as they walked to her front door. It was a high-rise, its walkway lined with fall flowers and pumpkins. At the top of the five steps, she turned around and looked down at him. "Care to come in and meet my parents?"

"Um, no. They might think that we're…well, you know what I mean. And I don't want to give them any false hopes about their daughter."

"Coward!" She laughed. "They already know how I am, so there's no jeopardy involved."

"I've got an early morning," he finally conceded. "I promised to take early-morning duty at the clinic and work straight through to close."

"That's being quite the martyr, isn't it?"

"It gives a couple people the opportunity to be off and have the day with their families, including you, if you want it."

"But the clinic can be a madhouse on Saturdays because, outside the ER, we're the only practice that's open on the weekends."

Simon shrugged. "Weekday, weekend, it's all the same to me. Otherwise, I'd be spending my day at home, alone, which gets boring after the first hour."

"I might drop in, depending on my parents' plans," she said, then, standing on the top step while he was two below her, she gave him a gentle kiss on the lips.

Nothing demanding, nothing deep and delving at first. Just a kiss between friends was the way she looked at it. Although the second kiss was more. It probed, and was a real kiss, not just a friendly one. And it went on forever, grew in intensity until she was nearly breathless. Her face blushed and her hands trembled as she tried to bid him a nonchalant good-night, which was nearly impossible to do given her rising feelings for him. So, he didn't want a woman with a child but she couldn't help the way she felt when she was around him, either, so what was she going to do?

"See you t-tomorrow," she stammered as her knees trembled on her way in the door. But before she could get inside he gave her a long, hard kiss.

This one deep and abiding. The kind of kiss reserved for dates and special occasions. The one that set her heart on fire.

Even though it was mid-October the chill in the air turned into a fiery blaze and it was all she could do to keep from fanning herself. But that would be too much of a giveaway. Too obvious a reaction to what should have been a simple kiss. So, instead she buzzed herself in and turned back to face him. "Oh, and, Simon, thanks for the lovely evening. I really did enjoy the time out with you." And the kisses. So very much the kisses.

"Glad you did," he said, backing away. One step down and he turned and sprinted to the sidewalk. "See you tomorrow...maybe."

She waited until he was out of sight before she stepped in and, once she'd greeted the concierge, she went on upstairs, which was where her mother practically pounced on her.

"He's quite a good looker," Mrs. Carson said.

"Were you looking out the window, Mom?" Del asked.

"Maybe for a minute. With your binoculars."

Del shook her head. "He's a friend. That's all. *A friend.*" Even though tonight he felt like more—so much more. And that second kiss was certainly for more than friends.

"He's a colleague," she said, feeling the blush rise once again in her cheeks. "That's all." Except colleagues didn't kiss colleagues the way he'd kissed her, or the way she'd kissed him back. Especially the way she'd kissed him back!

CHAPTER NINE

SHE WAS QUIET around Simon for the next couple of days. In fact she avoided him—something that wasn't lost on him. When they did make contact it was about work and that was all. Nothing personal, no references to two nights before, definitely no small talk. But what had he expected from Del, anyway? She was the original no-contact girl, and he wasn't acting much differently himself. No contact, nothing personal. And there was nothing *not* personal about their kiss on her front step. In fact, as kisses went, it was right up there with the best he'd ever had. Which wasn't good at all as he didn't want the relationship to blossom. Of course, he was hanging on to the hope that she didn't want it, either. So that made it two against the odds, which he liked a lot. Except he was afraid that one more kiss and he'd fall hard, since he was already halfway down.

So the days went on and he alternately regretted and was glad for that moment of intimate contact because it showed him that he could move on. He was no longer so emotionally strung out from his previous marriage, which was a good thing. But the bad thing was the distance that kiss had put between Del and him and he regretted that enormously as he had to work with her, and he also enjoyed her friendship. But he was finding that he wanted more, and the more he resisted it, the more he wanted it and couldn't stop thinking about it. That wasn't to say he wanted some convoluted, drawn-out high-tension relationship that would lead him back to where he didn't want to go. But he liked the conversation, liked the companionship and most of all liked it with Del. Though, as it stood, that moment was done. They'd given in to the weakness and look where it had got them.

Simon sighed as he entered Exam Four to take a look at a little boy who had a bad cough and a runny nose. Cute kid with curly red hair and green eyes, and a look that told Simon he was in agony. "So, what can I do for you today?" he asked the boy, as he acknowledged the boy's mother.

"Can you make me better?" Billy asked. "I don't feel so good."

"And where do you feel bad?"

He pointed to his head then to his throat.

"How long you been feeling bad, Billy?" he asked the boy, who was about eight. He liked to make direct contact with his patients when he could as he found that they had great insight into their own ailments—insight outside what a parent might report.

"Since day before yesterday."

"So which came first? The runny nose or the sore throat?"

The child shrugged. "Runny nose, I think."

Now Simon deferred to the mother. "Is that right?"

"He was running a slight fever day before yesterday, and the sore throat came on last night."

Simon smiled. "Thank you for getting him here so quickly. You'd be amazed how long it takes some parents to react when their child is sick."

And so the conversation and exam went for the next fifteen minutes until Simon diagnosed Billy with a mild head cold, and prescribed something for the stuffiness as well as the sore throat. Then the exam was over. Just like that he was alone in the exam room thinking about Del again. So much for the power of a good distraction, he thought as he headed back to the hub to hand-deliver the applicable notes and prescriptions to the checkout clerk. In that brief lull he saw Del dash down the hall, white coat tails flying, and it all came back to him. The conflict, the resolve, everything.

Face it. He wasn't sure what he was going to do about Del yet and, so far, he hadn't given any thought to the fact that this might be the end of something that had never really got started. So he liked Del! More than liked her, cared for her! But as what? A friend, a possible lover? And what was the big deal anyway? They were two mature adults who knew exactly what they wanted. What was stopping them from taking their relationship to another level and evening it out there rather than leave it festering where it was?

Fear, that was what. They'd both spoken their minds, made their opinions, fears and vulnerabilities perfectly clear, and that was that. But why couldn't they work through those issues together? Or could they? It seemed a logical thing to do, having some help to get through. But Del was afraid of that help and, to be honest, so was he. Because there was no telling where it would go. Vulnerability was a strange thing. It caused people to do things they didn't want; caused them to break vows and promises and ignore the real heart. So maybe Del was correct in ignoring this whole thing.

But, damn it! Why did he want to pursue it anyway?

It wasn't the fact that it was awkward so much as that she was embarrassed by the whole episode. She'd kissed him. Started it, and welcomed the second and third kisses. Then she'd avoided him ever since because she didn't know where to go from there. They'd established some kind of chemistry, obviously. But it was nothing she wanted to admit. She wasn't ready. She had Charlie to think about. And a job. No time to be in a committed relationship. The list was long and she'd gone over and over it all weekend and hauled it out and went over it again each and every time she saw him. He had that irresistible charm she needed to keep away from or else next time the third kiss would lead to more, and she couldn't handle that. Didn't want to handle it. All she wanted in her life right now was her son. So it was time to back all the way away and simply be professional colleagues.

Except she remembered those kisses; they were on her mind all the time. So was the next thing and the thing that could come after that if she allowed it. Which she wouldn't. Of course. The kisses were it and no further. It was fixed in her mind like etched glass.

"Do you think talking about it would help us?" he finally asked her.

"Talk about what?"

"What we were leading up to."

She frowned. "We weren't leading up to anything. They were just simple kisses, that's all."

"But what they evoked wasn't so simple, was it? We've been avoiding each other like the plague for the past two days and I know it has everything to do with that last kiss."

"It was a mistake."

"You weren't acting that way Friday night."

"I was out of character for myself."

"Or maybe that was in character and now you're out of character," he returned. As they walked along the hall, each on his or her way to visit a patient, there was no way she could get away from him for the next thirty seconds, so he took hold of her arm, an intimate gesture in and of itself, and led her to Exam Three, to treat a rash. "You enjoyed the evening, Del, and there's no denying that."

"I'm not denying it," she said, looking around to make sure no one else could hear their private conversation. Luckily, that end of the hall was empty of employees, and all the patients back there were in their rooms and would have to have ears pressed to the door to hear them. "It was a nice evening and it was nice to get out and have some adult company."

"We could do it again."

"No," she snapped. "We can't. We both know where this thing could go if we let it, and neither of us want it."

"That's not what your lips were saying."

"Lying lips."

Simon chuckled. "Beautiful, kissable lips."

"And *that's* the problem. I don't want to be kissed. It can lead to, well…other things. And I don't want that in my life right now. I'm doing good to manage everything I've already got without adding anything more."

"Would you even admit it if you wanted more?"

"Have you changed your mind, Simon? Have you suddenly decided that it's time to go out on the hunt again?"

"Not the hunt so much as I've decided it's time to move on."

She laid her hand on the door handle. "Well, I'm happy right where I am. And that's the difference between us. You can change your mind easily enough, but I can't. I'm on the course I want to be on."

"And you've never heard of adjusting the course?"

"Not in my life. Not since Charlie."

"Too bad, because I think we could have something." He bent low and stole a quick kiss, then left her standing all flushed and confused at her patient's door. It took her a few seconds to regroup before she went inside and was greeted by a mild case of the chicken pox. "Hello, Miranda," she said as she saw the little girl scratching away at the pustules on her arms. "I think I've got a cream that will help relieve the itching."

Too bad she didn't have a cream to relieve her of her growing feelings for Simon.

"Hello, dear," Del's mother said, greeting her at the door when she got home. "Your father's out for a stroll with

Charlie. Oh, and those came for you a little while ago." Gloria pointed to the dozen long-stemmed red roses all bedded together in a spray of white baby's breath. "I don't know who he is—maybe the man on your doorstep the other night—but he has good taste."

"He's one of the doctors at the clinic. Just a colleague."

"Colleagues don't send colleagues red roses if there's not something more attached to it."

"This colleague wants to take our friendship to the next level."

"Well," said her mother. "It's about time. Is he the one you went out with Friday night?"

"That was just a dinner among friends. That's all." OK, so it was a bit of a lie. But there was no reason to let her mother in on something that wasn't meant to be. She'd only get her hopes up that her stubborn daughter was giving in, which wasn't the case.

"And these are red roses among friends, too? Is he why you've been so grumpy these past couple of days? Honestly, that's why your father took Charlie for a walk over to the park. We're both aware of how grumpy you are when you come home from work, and he didn't want to deal with it this evening."

"OK," Del said, sighing. "I thought I'd found the perfect companion—someone who didn't want to get involved as much as I don't want to get involved. But things have changed. Now he...well. Let's just say that he wants to be the whole package when I'm still not in the mood to unwrap it."

"Because of Eric?"

"Because of Charlie and me. We have a good life."

"That could be so much better if you opened yourself up to letting someone in."

"That's your marriage, and maybe someday I'll find something like what you and Daddy have. But not now."

"And you're not the slightest bit interested in Dr. Red Roses?" her mother asked.

"I'm not saying I'm not interested. It's just that Simon wants to take things faster than I'm ready for."

"He's a man who knows what he wants."

"He wants me to fill a void left by his ex-wife and stepdaughter."

Gloria Carson took a step backward. "You didn't even read the card that came with the flowers." She grabbed it and handed it over to Del.

Del hesitated before she took it from her mother's hand. Suppose it spelled out some kind of term of endearment, or said something she didn't want it to.

"You're being silly, Del," her mother accused. "It's just a simple card. A small one. How many words could he have squeezed on it?"

"It's not how many, Mom. It's what they might say."

Her mother grabbed the card back and sat it down next to the flowers. "You're too stubborn for your own good. You know that?"

"It's just that I'm trying to do what's best for Charlie and me, and I don't think squeezing in a relationship is what either of us needs right now."

"Don't go using my grandson as your excuse. At his age he doesn't care one way or another. If there's something about this Simon that doesn't interest you, that's fine. There'll be another one come along. But you don't need any kind of excuse. If you want to, then do it. If you don't want to, then don't do it. But quit trying to fool yourself into believing that your son needs only you because he's at a perfect age to welcome others into his life. In fact, he's open to it much more than you are. So I'm not saying it has to be this Simon you work with, but at least keep yourself a little more open to the possibility that there's someone out there for you."

"It could be Simon," she heard herself admit, then wanted to kick herself for saying the words out loud.

Gloria arched her perfectly sculpted eyebrows. She was a striking lady—short blond hair, petite figure, eyes that told the whole story. "When I met your father I knew right away. No denying it for me as he was such a good catch I didn't want him single out there in the world for fear someone else would snap him up. But that's just me. I've always known what I wanted and gone out and got it."

"I know what I want," Del defended, as her gaze went to the flowers and the note sitting next to the vase.

"Doesn't sound like it to me. In fact, you sound a little lost."

"I'm not lost." Words spoken tentatively. "It's just that I'm not…"

"Found." Gloria crossed over and hugged her daughter. "Speaking of which, I'm going across the street to the park to find your father and finish off the walk with him. You're welcome to come along, or you can stay here and relax. And think of more excuses why you don't want to go after the one who could be the one."

She patted her daughter on the cheek, then grabbed a light jacket and headed to the door. "And don't worry about dinner. Your father and Charlie and I will find something on our walk."

"Tell Daddy to make sure Charlie is warm enough."

"Your father doesn't need to be told how to take care of a child. The one he raised turned out just fine. Except for that little glitch..."

Del laughed. "I don't have a glitch."

"Then it's a blind spot. Call it what you want."

Del shook her head, and sighed impatiently. "How long will you be gone?"

"Long enough," her mother said, laughing. "And not a moment longer than that." With that she walked out the door, leaving Del alone in her condo. It was strange being there all by herself. She was used to having Charlie around, to talk to, to fuss over. "So it's just me," she said aloud, feeling silly for talking to the walls.

She looked at the card next to the roses, and it was getting larger and larger. Or maybe it was that her attention was becoming more and more fixed on it. Whatever the case, she picked it up, looked at it, then put it back down. Then picked it up again, and held it up to the light as if something were going to be revealed in the overhead studio lamp suspended from her ceiling. Talk about feeling silly. She was certainly going to teach Charlie to be more direct than she was.

"Charlie..." she murmured, as she picked up the envelope yet again and finally looked at the note Simon had enclosed. It simply read *thank you*. But that made her wonder what he was thanking her for. Was it dinner, or the kisses at the door? Was it for something on the job, or for listening to his plight with Amy? In fact, the card wasn't even signed so the flowers could have been from anyone, which left her feeling a little disappointed. No, she didn't want more sentiment, but she did want to know why he was thanking her. And if the flowers were, indeed, from Simon.

On impulse, she picked up her cell phone and called his number.

"Simon Michaels," he came on, sounding as if he was in a rush.

She found it strange he didn't identify her with the phone-number-recognition feature on his own phone but maybe he was in too much of a hurry to look at it. "It's me," she said, in a subdued voice.

"As in Del?" he asked.

She could hear the teasing tone in his voice. "As in Del."

"And what can I do for you this lovely evening, Del?"

Now he was toying with her, which caused her to relax a little.

"Were you the one who had the flowers delivered?"

"Flowers, you say?"

"Flowers, I said. Red roses, white baby's breath. Ring any bells?"

"Oh, *those* flowers. I seem to recall picking them out this afternoon on my lunch hour."

"Why, Simon?"

"I thought they were pretty."

"They're beautiful. But you're evading my question. Why did you send them?"

"I think the card says it all. You *did* read the card, didn't you?"

"You mean the one with the very vague thank-you?"

"I don't see that as vague. In fact, I think it's pretty direct. I was thanking you."

"But for what?"

"Ah, now comes the real reason for the phone call. The lady wants to know what I'm thankful for."

"The lady *is* curious."

"You're acting like nobody's ever sent you flowers before."

"I've had flowers before, even from you, but I usually know why they've been sent."

He chuckled. "Not knowing bothers you, does it?"

"Well, if it's for the kiss…"

"Which kiss, specifically, as we're beginning to develop a habit?"

"It's not a habit!" she exclaimed. "And the one this afternoon…"

"Stolen kisses are often the best, don't you think?"

"So that's what you're thanking me for?" She'd hoped it was for something more than a pure physical urge. Maybe in the grand scheme of things she did want him to admit that his feelings for her were growing stronger, and the roses signified that. But they were for that silly little kiss at the exam-room door? Yes, she was disappointed. The thing was, she seemed to be wanting some big romantic gesture on one hand, and on the other she didn't. Which clearly indicated she was confused by the whole prospect of the man called Simon Michaels.

"What I'm thanking you for is a whole conglomeration of things—your friendship, your kisses do have some play in there, for being a great colleague..."

"And for not firing you when you manhandled me in the hallway today?"

"You looked at that as manhandling?"

"I looked at it as inappropriate."

"Then you've never watched any of the medical shows on television because they're always doing inappropriate things in empty rooms, halls, supply closets. X-ray is a particular hotbed of activity of that sort," he continued, then laughed. "Were you a woman of the world, you'd know."

"I am a woman of the world. I just didn't appreciate—"

"And here I was thinking you were calling me to thank me for the flowers. How disappointing that you turned it into an argument."

"You didn't even sign your name to the card."

"You've got that many men calling on you that it required my name?"

"You know I don't have *any* men calling on me. So what's this about, Simon?"

"Dinner tonight?"

She huffed an exasperated sigh into the phone. "You think food will fix whatever's ailing us?"

"What's ailing us, Del, is you. You're too suspicious. I invited you out for a simple dinner, and all that requires is a yes or no. Yet look what you go and do. You blow it up into something that it's not."

"But you're the one making advances."

"And you're the one rebuffing them. All I did was ask you out to dinner."

"You sent me flowers," she reminded him.

"For a totally separate reason, not to be confused with anything in the future."

"So you consider dinner tonight the future?"

"Well, it's certainly not in the past, is it? Especially since the evening is young. Oh, and I know you're alone because I ran into two people pushing a baby carriage with a baby in it who bears a striking resemblance to Charlie. Nice people, by the way. They asked me to accompany them to dinner."

"So let me guess. You told them you hoped to have other plans in the near future."

"Actually, they told me to call you and ask you to come along."

"Which you didn't do."

"Which I'm doing now."

"Because you knew I'd call you."

"Something like that." He chuckled. "And for what it's worth, I'm willing to take romance off the table this evening, if that's what you want. In fact, since you're so darned suspicious of them, I'll even take the flowers back."

"I'm keeping the flowers. And I'm not going out with you to have dinner with my parents."

"Then where would you rather go? Over to Maria's Italian Kitchen? That's always good."

"What's always good is a night alone with Charlie."

"Which you can't have because he has other plans."

"So what are we fighting about, Simon?"

"Nothing, as far as I'm concerned. I sent you some flowers and asked you out to dinner. You didn't thank me for the flowers and you haven't accepted my invitation. Does that about sum it up?"

"Did anybody ever tell you that you can be frustrating?"

"I've heard that said a time or two."

"So then it's not just me who thinks that?"

"Why would I admit something like that to you? We all have our peculiarities, you know."

"Mine being?" she asked, not sure she wanted to hear the answer.

"Your attitude. You're so...evasive. And you're sure as hell one of the most doubting people I've ever known. I mean, I sent you flowers and look at the way you're acting about it. You'd think I'd sent you something toxic instead of roses."

"Yes," she said.

"Yes, what?"

"Yes, dinner."

"Seriously?"

"Didn't you ask me?"

"I asked, but I didn't expect you'd accept."

"Do you want me to turn you down? Because I can."

"No. No. I asked, and I wanted you to accept. But with the way we are..."

"How are we, Simon? Tell me, how, exactly, are we?"

"If you know, you tell me, because I don't have a clue."

"Well, then, should I have said no?"

"You should have said exactly what you said. But

without all the bickering in between the question and the answer."

"How about we don't bicker tonight?" she asked him.

"No bickering. No romance. Anything else?"

"No more flowers."

"Then next time I should send chocolates?"

"I thought I'd order out and bring it home," he said when she arrived at his door later that evening. "Didn't know what you'd want so I have a sampler of several different dishes. I recalled you like Italian."

"I love Italian," she said, stepping into his condo. It was a converted warehouse, huge on space, and lacking furniture. But very esthetically pleasing. Immediately she began to decorate it in her head. Some easy chairs, a dining-room set, some bookshelves, a sofa… Right now all he had were a couple of chairs, a coffee table and a coat tree. "And I love this condo."

"Like I said, it's too much for me. I bought it with the intention of fixing it up for Amy, but now, since that's a no-go, I just haven't gotten around to doing anything with it."

"You could fit two of my condos in it. Charlie would love all the space."

"Really, at six months old? He's an advanced kid if he's that cognizant of the amount of space around him. Of course, babies are amazing little people, but I doubt the size of this place would really impress your son one way or another."

"Maybe in a few years."

He took her jacket and showed her to the counter in

the kitchen, where he'd laid out his array of food. "You feeding an army?" she asked.

"Depends on how hungry you are."

"I can tell you right now that I'm not that hungry. Looks like you're going to be eating Italian leftovers for several days."

"You and Charlie can always drop by and help me."

"Or I can always stay at home and feed Charlie something less messy."

"At his age, is there anything less messy?"

She laughed. "He doesn't quite have his table manners down yet. But we're working on that."

Simon pulled two plates from the cupboard and handed one over to Del, who was busy deciding what she was going to eat. "I opted out of spaghetti because that's too messy. But if you want spaghetti I can run back over there and..."

She held up her hand to stop him. "What you have here is fine. I'm always good with penne and garlic bread." With that she dished up a plate then stood and looked at him. "Where do you propose we eat this?"

"On the floor at the coffee table." He held up a bottle of wine. "It's red. Hope that's OK with you. I know you don't drink much but you've got to have wine with a fine Italian meal."

"Red's fine. And I'll take half a glass."

"It really does affect you, doesn't it?" he asked, pouring the wine.

"When you've seen what I've seen..." She shrugged. "I spent my whole pregnancy being so careful, not eating or drinking anything that wasn't good for my baby, not engaging in risky activities. I know you can't prevent all the misfortunes that can happen in birth but I sure tried hard to be as good as I could be. And my resolve not to drink…well, let's just say that, while I'm not against it, I don't see enough people exercising wisdom when it comes to what goes into their bodies."

"I'm sensing all the carbs in the Italian might not be the best thing I could have done."

"Carbs are fine. We need them. But I saw a pregnant woman the other day and she was smoking and I really wanted to tell her what she could be doing to her unborn child, but I stopped myself before I caused a scene and remembered that it's her right to smoke if she wants. It's not a good choice, in fact it's a lousy choice if you ask me, but she wasn't asking me."

"And the kids with FAS you treat—they're the reason you don't drink much."

"I got used to it in med school. My parents were never heavy drinkers—they'd have the occasional glass of wine but that was all. And as for me, the first time I saw a child with FAS I was glad I didn't drink too often as I would have given it up on the spot."

"I like a woman with conviction."

"I like a woman who controls her impulses," she said, on her way back to the living room, where she set her plate on the coffee table then sat cross-legged on the floor. "Or a man."

"You're referring to the kisses?"

"I might be."

"They were natural. A perfectly nice way to end the evening."

"What about the one you stole today?"

"I'll admit. I should have done better."

"You're kidding, aren't you?" she asked, reaching out to take her paper cup of wine.

"What if I'm not?"

"Then I probably shouldn't have come here."

He laughed out loud. "You're safe here, Del. Short of my getting drunk and manhandling you, you're going to be just fine."

"OK, so maybe that was a pretty strong word for what you did. I'm sorry that's the way I phrased what I think you see as a little innocent mauling," she said, then took a bite of her pasta.

"Mauling?"

She shrugged. "What else would you call it?"

"A kiss, pure and simple. A short, nearly circumspect kiss."

"Not circumspect enough."

"So it left an impression?" he asked.

"Not an impression so much as chapped lips."

"Whoa now. I wasn't there that long. If I'd really kissed you hard enough to chap your lips you wouldn't be eating tomato sauce with such gusto tonight. You'd be wincing between bites."

"I'm wincing on the inside."

"All this over one little stolen kiss. I wish now I'd made a production out of it. Swooped you into my arms, parted your lips with my tongue, run my hands over your…well, anything of yours would do fine."

She took another bite of her penne and shook her

head. "You'd better not be running your hands over anything of mine," she said after she swallowed.

"Isn't that why you're here? To get a little adult stimulation?"

"Adult, yes. Stimulation, definitely not."

Simon held up his paper cup for a toast. "Here's to not stimulating you, even though you know you want it."

She pulled her cup back from his. "What I want is to eat my dinner without being verbally assaulted."

"But I'm not assaulting you."

"You said you weren't ready for a relationship. That's why I've been keeping company with you. Because I took you at your word. Thought you were safe." She tore off a corner of the garlic bread and popped it into her mouth.

"But I am safe. And whether or not I'm ready for a relationship…honestly, I don't know. I tell myself I'm not, but when I'm with you…"

Del thrust out her hand to stop him. "No! Don't say it."

"Say what? That I'm attracted to you? Because I am."

"And I have a child."

"Which I'm fully aware of. That's the reason I'm not in this to commit to a serious relationship because I still mean what I said. No women with children. Not in the long-term."

"But short- or long-term, I'm a package deal and nothing about that's going to change."

"So we can't play at a flirtation?"

"Why bother?"

He set his paper cup down hard, and some of the

wine splashed out on the hardwood floor. "Damn it," he grunted, jumping up to run to the kitchen to grab a rag to clean up his spill. When he got back, Del was shrugging into her jacket getting ready to leave. "What's this about?"

"We won't work. We can play at it, or play around it, but that's still not going to make it something it isn't."

"So that second kiss. When you kissed me back, and I might add it was pretty hard, it didn't mean *anything* to you."

"It meant we were getting too close."

"Which is your cue to run away. Right?"

"I'm not running. I'm just avoiding the inevitable."

"By walking out my door."

"Look, Simon. We haven't got our wires crossed here. We both know what the other wants, so why tempt fate and broken hearts?"

"Because we do know what the other one wants."

"How does that make sense?"

He shrugged. "I had it all worked out in my head before you came over tonight. Thought we could actually get through a semi-romantic evening and end our day on a good note."

"Well, the part you hadn't thought through is that you're getting too close. If and when I ever meet a man I want in my life, I don't want him conditionally, and that's all you can be—conditional. You don't want a woman who has children and that's a huge condition. And I'm not saying that I want to be alone for the rest of my life because that's certainly not true. But I want a man who wants Charlie in his life, too, and who'll love my son as much as I do. That won't be you. It's not your fault, though. The thing is, as much as you try to fool yourself into a relationship with me, it just won't work because I'm not who you ultimately want."

"Which makes me not who you ultimately want."

"Does that make sense?"

"You want to know what makes sense?" he asked, taking a step closer to her.

He was so close she could smell the tinge of garlic on his breath. "This won't make it right for us, Simon," she said breathlessly.

"Who the hell cares what's right or wrong?" he said, his voice so thick with need it was almost a growl.

Dear God, she wanted this, and she wanted him, too. Just one time. Like their stolen kiss, a stolen moment of intimacy. In that very moment all her resolve just melted away—she forgot all the reasons why this wasn't the sensible thing to do and just gave in to her desires. She wanted Simon. Now.

"Do you have a bed?" she asked, twining her fingers around his neck. So what if they hadn't defined their friendship in terms of how it was going to be? She was an adult and she could certainly be adult about a one-time fling. Or maybe it would be more than once. Who knew? Who even cared at this point? It wasn't as if they were a couple of kids groping around in the backseat for a fast slap and tickle. They could do this…she could do this without regrets because she genuinely cared for this man. Maybe she was even falling in love with the type she said she'd never have a relationship with. It didn't really matter, though. None of it did. She wanted him here and now and she could tell he wanted her just as much. So, all things considered, what was one night out of her life? Not much, that was what.

"King sized."

"With sheets?"

"Just put on clean ones because I was hoping..." He bowed his head down to hers and pried her mouth open with his tongue, and delved in urgently.

The kiss was rough and demanding, like the one she'd been waiting for and had never before had. It was so full of need as he explored the recesses of her mouth and pulled her so tightly to him she could feel his erection pushing against her belly.

"Are you sure?" he panted as he removed her jacket.

"One time only," she said as her own breaths started coming in short bursts. "Read nothing into it, Simon," she said, as he picked her up and carried her to the bedroom.

"Hell, reading is the furthest thing from my mind." He threw her down on the bed and landed on top of her. "Oh, and so you know, once is never enough."

CHAPTER TEN

DEL WAS NAKED, basking in the steamy spray of the shower with Simon, not anxious to leave his condo, torn between the knowledge that she wanted to stay and couldn't, when his cell phone went off.

"I should probably take this," he said, reaching over to the vanity top to grab it. "Simon Michaels speaking," he said, as he playfully rubbed the palm of his hand over her right breast.

He listened for a second then dropped his hand from her breast, and said, "When?" His voice was dead serious. "How is she doing?" He listened for a minute and finally said, "I'll be there in twenty minutes… No, you're not interrupting anything. I *said*, I'll be there." With that he clicked off his phone and stepped out of the shower abruptly, leaving the cold air to flutter in behind him.

Goose bumps raised on her body. "One of our patients?" she asked, grabbing a towel and wrapping it around her as she stepped out. Simon was already half-dressed.

"No. It's Amy. She was in an accident tonight and

she's on her way to Lakeside right now. Yvette had her rerouted halfway across town so I could take care of her. Which I can't because I don't work in the hospital."

"Is it serious?" Del asked, running into the bedroom and dropping the towel to pull on her clothes.

"She's not conscious, and that's all I know."

She wanted to ask him if he needed her there, but that didn't mesh well with their new relationship—dragging a lover along to visit an injured little girl. So she followed him out the door, and down the flight of steps to the outside door, then onto the sidewalk. "If there's anything I can do…"

Simon shook his head. "I'll call you later." Then he was off in an abrupt run, no goodbye, no goodbye kiss. Nothing. She stood there for a second and watched him until he turned the corner, then she turned and walked toward her condo feeling quite…unresolved. Although it wasn't his fault. Amy was in trouble and his place was with her and Yvette.

Still, it was unsettling having him practically jump out of bed and into the arms of his ex-wife, no matter what the circumstances. Oh, well, she thought as she keyed herself into the building and said hello to the night concierge, who was sitting at the front desk reading a mystery novel. It was good while it lasted.

Very good. And best of all, come morning she wasn't going to kick herself because she'd wanted it just as much as he had. *I am human*, she thought, as she took one final appraisal to make sure every piece of her clothing was in perfect array before she entered her condo and was forced to confront her parents. Straightening her hair a little, and making sure her blouse was buttoned properly, she glanced at her watch. Two hours, all in. Not bad. Not bad at all. Especially for someone who'd started out the evening not even wanting a minute of it.

Del puttered around her condo for a while, folding Charlie's clothing, talking to her parents, all of it very restless energy. She knew where she needed to be and it certainly wasn't here.

"Why don't you go to the hospital and help your friend through this?" Her mother's suggestion was very much at the forefront of her thoughts, especially when she considered how he'd been there to help her when Charlie was sick. Simon hadn't left her side, and she wouldn't have gotten through it without him. But the thought that held her back was Yvette. She wasn't sure she wanted to see him with his ex, as that would remind her that Simon was at one time part of a happy little family group, even though she knew that wasn't the case now. But a badly injured child had a way of making people grow closer and, having just been in his bed, she wasn't sure she could go that route this soon after.

"He was a big help to me," she told Gloria, who was getting Charlie ready for bed.

"Then go to him, dear. I'm sure he'll be glad to see you."

But she felt a little strange running after him when just an hour ago they'd forgotten for a few minutes there was an outside world for them to worry about. But she had to behave maturely about this, didn't she?

Simon might need her. And she was pulled toward him as she paced her condo, going back and forth from wall to wall. "Look, do you mind watching Charlie for the night? I think I need to be with Simon right now."

"Of course we don't mind watching Charlie, do we, Charles?"

Charles Carson smiled. "I'll walk you over to the hospital."

"I'll be fine on my own."

"You may be thirty-five, but you're still my little girl and my little girl gets her father's escort to the hospital even though it's only a couple blocks away."

Del nodded. Now wasn't the time to argue with her father. She just wanted to get to the hospital. So she threw on a lightweight jacket and waited for him at the front door. "I'm glad you're both here," she said, giving her mother a hug. "It makes life easier. And Charlie loves having you here."

"Not as much as we love being here with him," her mother said. "Now, you go on and take all the time you need. Charlie will be just fine with us."

Del's dad opened the door for her and took hold of her arm as they entered the hallway and went to the elevator to wait. "You like this fellow a lot, do you?" Charles asked her.

"We're friends."

"Last time we checked you were colleagues."

"Things change. And he's been a big support to me, especially when Charlie got sick."

The elevator door opened and they got in and rode

down to the first floor. "He was there for me every step of the way. I didn't even have to ask him."

"And the two of you are dating now?"

Dating and so much more, but that wasn't something she cared to discuss with her dad. "We've had a couple of dates. Nothing fancy. Just…nice."

"He's not like Eric, is he? Someone who'll string you along with his promises for years, and cheat on you every chance he gets."

"Simon and I don't have that kind of relationship. It's casual. If he dates someone else…" she tried to imagine Simon with another woman and her heartbeat increased a beat or two "…that's his business. Like I said, we're just casual friends."

"Well, casual or not, don't go getting yourself mixed up in another screwy situation like you had with Eric. He was no good for you."

That was putting it mildly. "What Simon and I have can hardly be called a relationship, Dad. So don't worry about me. I've got my head screwed on straight this time."

The rest of their two-block walk they talked about Charlie and the progress he was making. Then when they arrived at the hospital, Charles left Del at the admitting door and turned around and walked home, while Del's stomach knotted. This was where she got involved in a whole different way than she'd ever believed would happen and it scared her. But, this was about Simon and his stepdaughter, and they might need her help. At the least, Simon could use the support. So, turning toward the ward, she wandered down the hall, took a look at the admittance board in the emergency room and saw that Amy was in holding in Trauma Five. Which meant Yvette couldn't be too far away. Gulping, she slipped very quietly into Trauma Five and just stood pressed to the wall.

"Amy, honey, you're going to be just fine."

"I'll swear, that truck came out of nowhere," Yvette said. She was standing at the bathroom mirror fixing her hair.

Simon could smell the liquor on her breath and the stale cigarettes in her hair. So she'd picked up a new bad habit. Nothing like some secondhand smoke for Amy.

"What was she doing in the street in the first place? And at this time of night?"

"I was going to the store, and I had her run back to the house to get my purse. I'd forgotten my credit card."

"And she crossed the street alone?"

"She knows how to cross the street, Simon." Yvette slid into a chair and almost slid down to the floor, she was so *relaxed.* "I know you taught her."

"Of course I taught her, but I didn't teach her how to do it alone, after dark, on a busy street."

"It was an accident. And if that damn truck hadn't turned the corner when it did…" She waved a limp hand in the air. "It was all his fault. You should be talking to him."

"Did he stop after he hit her?"

"He stopped, and accused me of being a bad mother. Of all the nerve."

Simon shut his eyes for a moment. "Where's your husband?"

"Away on business," she said.

"Did you call him?"

"Why? Amy isn't *his* kid."

"And she's not my kid, either, but you called me."

"Because you can patch her up and see that she gets home."

"She's unconscious, Yvette. That's going to take a hell of a lot more than a patch."

"Maybe Yvette would like some coffee," Del said from the doorway.

Simon spun around to see her standing there with a paper cup full of coffee from the vending machine.

"I saw how she was and I thought..." She shrugged and held out the coffee. "Do you want anything, Simon?"

He shook his head no, then took the cup from Del and handed it to Yvette. "Drink it!" he ordered her.

"You know I like sugar in mine."

"I'll go get sugar," Del volunteered, and in a split second was out in the hall on her way to the bank of vending machines, with Simon on her heel.

"Why are you here?" he asked, his voice still hanging on to a shred of its accusatory tone.

"Thought you might need me. And I do have some clout here."

"What I need is information about Amy," he said, running a nervous hand through his still-mussed hair. He hadn't combed it after their shower together.

"She's going into X-ray right now. Still unconscious." She shrugged. "I looked at her chart before I came down here."

"She was hit by a truck."

"I know. And the police aren't holding the driver because it was an accident. Amy crossed against the light. Apparently her mother was across the street screaming at her."

"Damn," he muttered, fixing on the sugar packets in Del's hand. "She must have gotten confused."

"Or frightened, poor thing."

"Is Charlie OK?"

"He's with my folks. They'd put him to bed before I got home." She reached out and took his hand. "Look, Simon. She's in good hands here. It's a small hospital but the staff is top-notch all the way around and they'll take good care of Amy."

"I should have fought harder for her. Should have gone back to court another time."

"You did everything you could do. And when she's older I think Amy will understand that. But in the meantime, I think you'd better go take care of Yvette. She's not in very good shape." Del placed the sugar packets in Simon's hand and closed his hand around them. "I'll go see what I can find out and I'll be back to talk to you directly."

He bent down and kissed Del on the forehead. "Thank you for coming. I know I was a little abrupt when I left you on the sidewalk, but—"

"But nothing. You did what any good parent would do. And I don't blame you. We all have ups and downs, especially when your children are sick or injured." She turned and reentered the trauma wing while Simon went to the waiting area only to find Yvette sound asleep, her head on the shoulder of the stranger sitting next to her. He was drinking her coffee. No sugar.

"She's awake now and they said you can go in and see her for a minute," Del told Simon, who was standing out in the hall leaning against the wall.

"Did they give you her diagnosis?"

"No, I thought that it would be better if they talked to you *and* Yvette, since you can't make the decisions for Amy."

"Don't remind me," he grumbled as he walked through the trauma doors into the main hall, with Del walking shoulder to shoulder with him.

"She's in a serious condition, Simon," Del warned. "Pretty beat up on the outside with some internal injuries, as well."

He nodded, and greeted the doctor on call, who was looking at Amy's EKG tracing as Simon stepped into the cubicle.

"Daddy," Amy said weakly. "I'm scared."

"Daddy's here to take care of you now. No need to be afraid," Simon said gently, taking hold of Amy's hand. She was dwarfed by the chest tube, EKG leads, IV tubing and oxygen mask on her, and Simon's first reaction was to assess everything, including blood that was coming out of one of the tubes. "So what are we talking about here?"

"She needs emergency surgery," Dr. Ross said, "to remove her spleen. We also need to surgically repair her leg. Her head films are negative for brain damage and she's alert and reactive."

"Daddy?" Amy whimpered. "I don't feel so good. Is Mommy going to be mad at me for messing up her evening?"

"Mommy's not mad. She's worried."

"I didn't mean to get hit, and I didn't see that truck. Honest I didn't." Amy coughed and a little bit of blood trickled out her nose.

"I'll go wake up her mother and get permission for the surgery," Simon said.

"How about you stay here and I'll go wake her up?" Del offered.

"She can be pretty ugly when she wakes up from a drink."

"And I can be pretty insistent." Del smiled as she squeezed Simon's arm. "You stay here and comfort your little girl. She needs you more than Yvette does."

"Thanks," he said, hovering over Amy's bed as the child drifted off to sleep.

"Why's she drifting in and out?" Simon asked the attending physician.

"We gave her something for pain and she's pretty sensitive to it."

"So tell me the truth. Is she going to be OK?"

"I'd like to get her spleen out of her as soon as possible, to control the internal bleeding. We're not too worried about her leg. It should repair pretty easily once we get the orthopedics team in place."

"Will she be able to endure that much surgery all at once?"

"We'll have to evaluate that as we go along," Dr. Ross explained.

Damn, he felt helpless. He wasn't her real dad, and he didn't even feel much like a real doctor at the moment. The worst part was, he couldn't make the decisions. By all legal rights he shouldn't even be here since Yvette had a restraining order out on him. But he didn't care about that. If they rounded him up and threw him in jail for being at his daughter's bedside, so be it. This was about Amy now, and Amy needed him here. From the looks of Yvette, so did she.

Out in the hall, Del looked into the waiting room at the sleeping woman who was slumped all over the man sitting next to her. She knew they weren't together and could only surmise this was Yvette in her drunken-stupor, passed-out state. It wasn't going to be easy to shake her out of it. "Yvette," Del called from the doorway.

Yvette lifted her head for a moment, then crashed back down on the willing stranger, who didn't seem to mind having her there. Living vicariously, Del thought as she stepped inside the crowded room. "Yvette, wake up."

"I'm awake," she mumbled, opening her eyes.

"You need to get up and come back to Trauma with me. Amy needs you."

"Kid doesn't even understand a stupid traffic light," she said, her voice slurring.

"Amy needs you," Del repeated as all eyes in the room turned to her.

"Her dad is with her."

"No, Simon is with her and you made sure he's not her dad, so he can't sign off on what Amy needs."

The man next to Yvette pushed her upright. "Your kid needs you, lady," he said.

"Fine. Tell Simon to sign the papers for me."

"He can't!" Del crossed the room and physically pulled Yvette from her chair. "You have to do that."

"I faint at the sight of blood," she complained. "Never could understand Simon and his passion for medicine 'cause you get exposed to all kinds of nastiness."

Del steadied the wobbly woman, and pulled her out into the hall. "She's in Trauma Five. Go down to the nurses' hub and sign the papers then go down to see Amy in Room Five. She needs to see you."

"And just who are you?" Yvette asked, straightening herself up.

"I'm a friend of Simon's."

"So he's got a girlfriend." She laughed a shrill laugh that could be heard the entire length of the hall. "Well, what do you know about that?"

"What I know is that you're wasting precious minutes of Amy's life. You need to go down there and sign the surgery consent form."

"OK. OK. I'll sign it, but I expect Simon to stay here with the kid while I go home and make myself presentable for my husband. He's coming home tonight."

"Honestly," Del hissed, "I don't care what you do after you sign the papers. In fact, I'll be glad to call you a cab."

"I'll just bet you would." Yvette snorted as she bobbed and wove her way down the hall, where she stopped at the central hub to inquire about the paperwork.

The unit secretary handed her a consent form, on which she scrawled a signature halfway over the entire page, then she turned and staggered back to the trauma doors.

"Your cab will be here in five minutes," Del told her.

"I don't suppose you're paying for it, too, are you? See, I don't have enough cash on me right now to..."

Del huffed out an impatient sigh as she took hold of Yvette's arm and led her to the door. The cab was already there, waiting, so Del got Yvette inside and handed the driver a hundred-dollar bill. "That's to make sure you get her up to her door," she said. Whatever happened after that, Del didn't care.

"How did you manage with Yvette?" Simon asked Del after Amy was taken down to surgery.

"Let's just say that she probably won't even remember any of it tomorrow."

"I appreciate everything you've done, up to and including sending her home."

"Amy doesn't need a drunken mother here."

Simon smiled as he took Del's hand and led her back to the cubicle where Amy had been treated. "She's going to spend the night in the ICU and if all goes well be transferred to a pediatric bed in the morning."

"Well, for what it's worth, I can see why you didn't stay with Yvette."

"Yvette does have her bad moments but she's not always so...oblivious. And she's not so cruel that she'd want to see her daughter hurt."

"But she's drunk!"

"Which means something's going wrong in her life."

He was much more lenient with Yvette than Del expected him to be. Did he harbor leftover feelings for her? Maybe part of him still loved her in some odd, convoluted way. It was obvious that Yvette still counted on Simon to see her through and Del felt confused by the emotional interplay she saw. Simon should have been livid with Yvette yet he wasn't. In fact, he was being awfully kind.

"She's worse now than she used to be. For all her faults, Yvette was never a real drunk."

"This new marriage must not be agreeing with her too well, then."

He shook his head. "And Amy's trapped in the middle of it."

"Might be a good time to revisit the custody issue. You'll have the records from the hospital to back you up." Del smiled sadly as he put his arm around her shoulder. "I'm sorry it turned out this way."

"So am I. Amy doesn't deserve this."

"Look, Simon. Let's go up to the doctors' lounge and sit there until Amy's out of surgery. I'll tell them at the desk where we'll be. They need to clean up this cubicle for the next patient."

Simon nodded his agreement and they walked, clinging to each other, to the elevator, where they boarded and went up one floor to the doctors' lounge. It was blessedly quiet in there. A couple of the docs there were dozing, one was eating a meal and another one was reading, with his reading glasses poised on the end of his nose. All in all, it was a peaceful place and Simon was glad for the quiet as he didn't feel like talking, he was so numb with worry. So he and Del sat on the couch, arms wrapped around each other, with Simon's eyes glued to the clock.

Every now and again he sighed and shifted, but he didn't let go of Del. It was well into the first hour of surgery when he finally spoke. "If I went after custody now, wouldn't it seem like I'm taking advantage of a bad situation? I'm afraid that would eventually hurt Amy. I should have had her with me, but the court has been against me every step of the way," he whispered, so as not to disturb the tranquil atmosphere in there.

Del nodded. "Sometimes life's just not fair. Tonight it's not fair for Amy."

He looked down at her and smiled. "Charlie's a lucky little boy having you for his mother. You were meant to have children, Del. I'll admit, I wondered why you wanted to do it, but now I know. You're a natural."

"Thank you," she said. "I love being a mother. I never gave it much of a thought while I was in med school, and even in the beginning of my practice, but being around babies every day…it's how I define myself now, even more than I've always defined myself as being a doctor. But I think you're a natural, too."

"A father without a child."

"Because the child's mother doesn't care enough about her to do what's right. I can't believe she wanted to go home before Amy's surgery."

"Believe it. That's the way the last couple years of our marriage were. She was out playing while I was at home taking care of Amy."

"Yet you still defend her."

"Because for all her faults, I know she does love Amy. It's just difficult for her because she doesn't have that natural mommy instinct like you do."

There he was defending Yvette again. She'd just made love with this man and here he was defending the woman she'd thought he hated. Perhaps it was her own judgment that should be called into question here, getting involved with a man who was distanced from the relationship because he still had feelings for another woman. Could she overcome that? Or did she even want to try?

"I'm just amazed that she wanted custody, when she clearly doesn't care about being a mother."

He shrugged. "I think having a child makes her appear more stable than she is. Yvette's a total mess. Worse tonight than I've ever seen her before."

"I can only imagine what her husband's like," Del commented.

"I've tried not to think about it," Simon said, sounding so discouraged his voice barely broke through the air around them.

"Simon, Del..." A scrub nurse entered the room. "Her splenectomy went fine. They're in for the leg repair now and Dr. Ross said to tell you he'll be up here in a little while to have a talk with you."

Simon heaved a sigh of relief. One surgery down, one to go. Which meant it was still a long night ahead of them. "Thank you," he told the scrub nurse, then turned to Del. "If you want, you can go home now. I'm fine here by myself. And little Charlie may be waking up wanting his mommy anytime."

"How about I call home and if I'm not needed there I'll stay here with you?"

"I'm really OK being by myself here. Especially since you did my dirty work and dealt with Yvette."

"Do you think you should call her with a progress report?" Del asked.

"How about I wait until she calls me?" he snapped.

"Because you're better than that."

"I know. And something's obviously wrong in her life or she wouldn't be acting the way she did. But I'd sure like to treat her the way she deserves."

"Except you won't, and you know it."

Simon sighed. "I'm not looking forward to calling her, but maybe by now she'll be coherent enough to care a little."

While Del made her call, only to find out that everything was being managed quite well, Simon made his to a voice mail message, telling the caller to call back in the morning. *"If you're calling at night, call back in the morning when I'm awake. If you're calling during the day and I don't answer, leave a message and I'll get back to you as soon as I can."*

Damn, she sounded so sweet on the phone. He could see why he'd fallen for her. She had a way of turning it off and on to suit her needs.

"So, what did she say?" Del asked.

"Nothing. It rolled over to voice mail."

"Seriously? With her child in surgery? Maybe she didn't want to be here but you'd think she'd want to know what was going on."

"She doesn't care."

Del frowned. "I just don't understand it."

"And I hope you never do. People like that shouldn't have children, and Yvette certainly is one of those people."

"Well, for what it's worth, my parents said to tell you that Amy is in their thoughts and prayers tonight, and they're keeping a good thought for you, too."

"Are you going home?"

She shook her head. "I'm here for the duration. As long as you need me..."

"Daddy, where am I?" Amy asked.

"You're in the recovery room. The doctors had to operate on you tonight and you're going to be just fine."

"Is Mommy here?"

"Mommy had a headache and she had to go home."

"Oh," Amy replied, her speech thick with anesthesia. "I'm so sleepy."

"Then go back to sleep, sweetheart."

"Are you going to stay here with me?"

"I'm not going to leave your side," he promised. "And next time you wake up I'll be right here, holding your hand."

"Promise?"

"Promise." He bent over and gave her a kiss on her forehead, then looked at her tiny form lying under the blanket. The daughter he would choose...if the choice were his to make. Unfortunately, it wasn't and he was scared to death that once she was past this crisis Yvette would take Amy away from him again.

Simon didn't know how he'd survive that.

"She looks like an angel," Del said, stepping up behind Simon and putting her hand on his shoulder.

"She is an angel. Such a good child… Yvette doesn't know what she has or how lucky she is."

"Well, Yvette is out in the waiting room with a man I take to be her husband. He's older. Old enough to be her father, and he looks like a dude, with all his gold chains and rings. And he's wearing sunglasses even though he's inside the building at night."

"He brought her here?"

Del shrugged. "She seems more sober than she did when I sent her home several hours ago."

"I suppose I should go out and see her."

"Well, they won't let her in Recovery. I told her she'd have to wait until Amy went to the ICU, then she'd probably get ten minutes with her."

"Was she agreeable?"

"Her husband did all the talking for her. He wanted to know when that would be and I told him we have no way of knowing. He wasn't happy to hear that."

"I guess it has to be done." Frowning, Simon stood up and walked slowly to the door, then out to the surgery waiting room.

"How is she?" Yvette asked as she looked in a compact mirror and fiddled with her hair.

"Rough shape. She lost her spleen, and had to have orthopedic surgery. She'll probably be down about six weeks, and they'll get her up and start her on physical therapy as soon as possible so she won't get weak."

"Six weeks?" Yvette's husband shouted. "We can't have a sick kid hanging around that long. We've got things to do, and if she's laid up that means we'll have to get someone to watch her."

"You must be Mack Brighton," Simon said, without extending his hand to the man.

"Sure, this is my husband, Mack," Yvette said. "Mack, this is my ex, Simon. The one who was fighting me for Amy."

"So you're the one who wants the kid. Funny how that's going to work out for you, 'cause it looks like you're going to get her for a while, since we can't take care of her the way she needs. Or, I suppose we could put her in a nursing home of some sort if you don't want her the way she is now."

"Amy's not going to a nursing home," Simon said, fighting hard to hold his temper in check.

"Then you'll keep her?" Yvette asked hopefully.

"Of course I'll keep her. But you'll have to have the court revoke the restraining order against me."

"And you'll have to give him full custody so he can make all her medical decisions," Del said from behind Simon. She stepped around him and looked straight at Mack. "The way it stands now, Simon can't do anything to help Amy because of the way you've got him tied up. So untie him and give him a full-custody agreement, then you won't have to have him bothering you every time something has to be decided."

"Sure, whatever," Mack grunted. "I'll call the attorney first thing in the morning."

"You're taking my baby?" Yvette asked, as if she wasn't even paying attention to the conversation going on around her. "Does that mean you're going to pay for her, too?"

"Of course I'll pay for her."

"And he won't come after you at some time in the future if you agree to sever all ties to Amy now, and in the years to come."

"You mean you're just going to take my baby away from me forever?"

"That's exactly what he means," Del interjected.

"And I want to adopt her," Simon said. "Give her my name and become her legal father."

"That's being harsh," Yvette said. "Just because she had a little accident."

"An accident that almost killed her," Simon returned.

"Let him have the kid," Mack said. "If you don't she's going to cost you a fortune, and don't expect me to chip in for her care."

"Why do I feel like you're all trying to take advantage of me?" Yvette asked, putting on her pouty face.

"You think you can do better?" Mack asked.

"You know I can't do better than you, babe," Yvette answered him.

"Then give him the kid. You don't want her anyway. You told me so a dozen times."

"Yet you went after me and took a restraining order against me having any contact with her?" Simon almost shouted.

"That was purely a strategic move," Yvette said. "And you failed."

"You were going to extort money from him to see his stepdaughter?" Del asked. "Was that the plan?"

"Not extort money so much as just make him pay for the privilege."

"I sure as hell don't pay for that kid," Mack butted in. "And I made that perfectly clear when we got married that the kid was baggage."

"Baggage her mother thought she could make a buck on," Del argued.

"Who the hell are you anyway, lady?"

"She's the person who cares more about Amy than Amy's mother does," Simon told him.

"Your hook-up?" Mack asked.

"My friend."

With that Del stepped closer to Simon and slid her hand into his. "His very good friend."

"Then you tell your very good friend he can have the kid if he wants her, but it's going to cost him."

"It will cost me nothing," Simon said, squeezing Del's hand. "In fact it will save me another court battle where I go after child support from Yvette, which is what I could do since you're so willing to give Amy away. I'm sure the courts would agree with me that neither of you deserves to have her, and if it gets that far in the court system Yvette might be the one who ends up paying me child support."

"You wouldn't do that," Yvette said. "We were married five years and the one thing I know about you, Simon, is that Amy matters more than anything else to you. You wouldn't tie her up in a family court battle like one that is bound to hurt her."

"You're right. I wouldn't. But you would, and that's the difference between us, Yvette. You'd use Amy and I'd protect her."

Del smiled. "See, the thing is, Amy will be going where she's loved and wanted, and if you care for Amy at all, then you'd want that for her. Especially since you'll be getting Mack in the deal."

Yvette sighed. "Are you going to be around to help raise her?"

"I'll be around," Del said, then looked up at Simon. "One way or another."

"Could I at least see her sometimes, Simon?"

Del held her breath. This whole thing had been a gamble to start with, but it looked as if Yvette was about to give in to her husband's wishes. Here was hoping she had no more children in the bargain.

"Of course. Ideally, you'd even want to have a relationship with her."

"Except we're moving out of Chicago," Mack said.

"We are?" Yvette questioned.

"Yep. I've got a hot prospect coming up in Vegas and I need to be closer to my work. Ain't no place for no kid, either."

"I could call."

"You can call," Simon agreed.

"And video conference," Yvette suggested.

Simon agreed to that, too, knowing full well that once Amy was out of her sight she'd also be out of mind. "So, I'll get an attorney. For my side of it, and—"

"Got one already," Del interrupted. "He's my next-door neighbor."

"Then it's set. I'll adopt Amy." It seemed so simple and almost civilized. Of course, they were talking money at this juncture and Yvette didn't have a say in that, apparently.

"And we won't be paying for the kid one way or another," Mack said, smiling as if he'd just won a great victory.

"And you won't be paying for the kid," Simon agreed, nodding. "Oh, and in case you're interested, Yvette, she did ask for you."

Yvette looked shocked. "You tell her Mommy's moving, that she'll be calling her as soon as she's settled in."

"You could see her before you go," Del suggested.

"Don't have time," Mack said. "We've got packing to do. Just make a lawyer's appointment before we leave town next week, and we'll get this all wrapped up."

"Dr. Michaels," one of the recovery nurses said, tapping Simon on the shoulder. "Just thought you'd want to know that Amy's coming round again and if you want to keep your promise to her..."

Simon took one last look at Yvette and, while he didn't regret their marriage because it had given him Amy, he did regret that she'd let herself be trampled so low. But that was her life, and he had a brand-new life ahead of him. "Thanks," he whispered as Mack and Yvette walked away. Simon didn't know if it was his imagination, or if it was real, but as Yvette glanced back he thought he saw a look of regret on her face. He hoped, for Amy's sake, he did. But Yvette was pulled into Mack's embrace as they exited the hall, and she didn't look back again.

"Goodbye and good riddance," Simon said as he rushed back to the recovery room, pulling Del along with him. By the time Amy came around again, he was sitting next to her, holding her hand with his left, and holding on to Del for dear life with his right.

Things had worked out rather simply, Del thought as she stood there. But she still wondered about Simon. Would he commit to someone other than Amy? If, per chance, they got together, how would Charlie rate with him? Would Charlie always come in second? She pictured him adoring Amy while practically ignoring Charlie, and that bothered her. She couldn't be involved with a man who would do that. Time would tell, she supposed, and if there was one thing she had plenty of, it was time.

"That's all for the night," Del said as she and Simon walked away from the ICU viewing window. "You can see her again in the morning."

"This has been the longest night of my life," Simon said, stretching his arms as he turned and started down the hall. He reached over and took hold of Del's hand. "Congratulate me. I'm going to be a father."

"Since I've known you, you've never not been a father," she said.

"You got pretty feisty in the confrontation." They walked past the exit sign and on to the front door. "I've never seen that side of you before."

"That's the mother side of me fighting for a child. Tonight I was fighting for Amy."

"But you're not her mother."

"And you were in the position where you had to be more diplomatic than I was. One wrong word and Amy would have been chucked into a nursing home while Yvette and Mack went to Vegas. So as the innocent bystander..."

"You're not so innocent, Del. Let me tell you, I have a new appreciation for that side of your motherhood. Pity the poor idiots who try to get one over on Charlie, because you've got some wicked claws."

She laughed. "It's called a mother's defense mechanism."

They headed out into the parking lot and decided to spend the rest of the night next door in the clinic so they'd be close to the hospital in case Simon was called back. Not that there was much left of the night, as it was going on to four a.m.

"I wonder if I'll develop something like it."

"Oh, I think you already have. You stand up for Amy quite nicely. Nice enough that it got you a child tonight."

"I don't think that's sunk in yet. More than likely it won't until I see the signatures on the court document."

She stopped and pulled him over to her, and reached up and kissed him full on the lips. "That's for good luck."

"I've already had all the good luck I'll ever need," he said, putting his arm around her waist as they finished their walk over to the clinic. "And it's sure been one hell of a night, you know that?"

"I know," she said, remembering how it had started

in bed. Just for a quickie was what she'd promised herself, except somewhere in there that quickie had been extended into an emotional commitment. She realized then that she did love Simon, and she didn't regret that for a moment. Loved the way he took care of his child, loved the way he was with her. Too bad he still wouldn't commit to another woman with a child because she was suddenly in the mood to be committed to him. But that just wasn't to be and she knew that. Couldn't blame him, either, after what he'd gone through with Amy. Besides, Amy would be enough for him to deal with for a good, long time.

Del sighed. Their timing was sure off, she decided. Which didn't make them too much of a meant-to-be proposition. It was on that note that she decided to leave him alone at the clinic and go on home, where she was supposed to be. At least in the morning she could see Charlie, and he would renew her vitality. Because tonight she felt fully drained. Fully, completely drained.

"She's doing great," Simon said. "She's in physical therapy next door so I decided to run over here to the clinic to see how things were going." He was on an extended leave of absence, pending Amy's release from the hospital any day now. And although he was officially offf call, he'd managed to drop in on Del at least once a day for the past two weeks. Sometimes he had a legitimate excuse, sometimes he just came to loiter and be near. Either way, she always seemed glad to see him. Glad, yet back to the casual. So while they hadn't managed another night together yet, that connection was still there between them, ever clinging. But he felt it slipping away.

Besides, Del's parents had gone home to Costa Rica and she was back to her old schedule, which left her with very little time to herself. "I've checked in on her a few times when I've gone over to visit Charlie on my lunch hour and she's wonderful. So bright. So eager to work hard to get better because she wants to come home and live in her new daddy's condo."

Simon smiled. "I can see why you didn't want to leave Charlie. It's a hard adjustment to make."

"It's getting easier when I drop him off, but it's never totally easy."

"Have you ever thought about a child-care center here in the clinic? We've got a few parents here who could benefit from that."

"Actually, no. I'd never thought of it, but it might be worth considering."

"That would keep Charlie closer to you. And Amy closer to me before and after school."

"So you're really going to come back to us when she's better?"

"Yes. I'd never planned on quitting altogether. Somebody's got to support us. So unless I marry a rich woman who doesn't mind taking on all the responsibilities…"

"She can't have children," Del reminded him.

"About that. I think I've changed my mind."

"Changed your mind about what?"

"About someone with children. I think I could possibly manage to have a relationship like that in my life."

"How? When all I've ever heard from you is that you wouldn't get permanently involved with a woman who has a child. When did that change, or did it change?"

"It changed when I started using my head. And it's about finding the right relationship. Knowing that she would love Amy as much as I would love her child."

"So you mean a blended-family type of situation?"

"That's what they're calling it these days."

"But could you do that, Simon? Just walk into a family and love her children as much as you love Amy? Or would Amy always come first? Because that wouldn't be right. Children need love on their own terms, and they don't need it in a pecking order. Amy comes first, the other child comes second." She shook her head. "It wouldn't work."

"But what if I didn't have that pecking order? If I accepted all the children as they are and loved them in no particular order?"

"You've gone to hell and back for Amy. How could she not come first in your life? I mean, you bring with you, by default, a split family already."

"Not split. Just blended."

Del blinked hard. "Anybody in mind?"

"Just one person. But I'm not sure she wants a relationship with anybody other than her son."

"I think she does. Something tells me she had a change of heart somewhere along the way. But you scare her because of your close ties to your daughter. Can anyone else truly fit in or will there always be a division? And while we're on the subject, do you still have feelings for Yvette?"

"I'll always care about Yvette because she's Amy's mother. But does that mean I want her back? Hell, no! I want to stay as far away from the woman as I possibly can. As for that division, we wouldn't be divided, Del. I don't worry that you couldn't love Amy as much as I do because I know your heart. As I hope you know mine."

"It still scares me, Simon. I'd love to have a daughter and Amy's a wonderful little girl I've already grown to love. But you...you're the unknown to me. Could you ever love Charlie the way I do? Because you'd have to before I...committed to anything. And I just don't know."

"What tripped me up?" he asked.

"Your own words, that you won't have a woman who has a child. I know that's not playing fair using them against you at this stage of our relationship, and especially now that you have your daughter, but it scares me that Charlie will always run a distant second to Amy, and I can't have that."

"Yet you don't think that Amy will run a distant second to Charlie?"

Del shook her head. "I have room in my heart for many more children. Amy would just fill in one of those empty spaces."

"Yet you don't think I could do the same for Charlie?"

"Blending isn't easy, is it?"

"What if I were to adopt Charlie and give him my name as my legal son instead of my stepson?"

"You'd want to do that?"

"In a heartbeat, if you'd let me, and if it would prove to you that I could love him as much as I love Amy. Stop and think, Del. Amy is not my biological child, either, yet I'd defy anyone who said she's not my daughter. I fell for her just the way I'm falling for Charlie."

"Then that makes you a remarkable man," Del said.

"So if I'd ask you to move in to my much larger condo…"

"I might be willing to accept. Provided you really want to take on another woman's child again and maybe add two or three more to the mix."

"More kids?"

She shrugged. "I like being a mother."

"Well, Amy could use another child in the house. She'll make a super big sister, and I could certainly use a woman who would stand by me as staunchly as you do."

"That's a mighty tall order."

"From a man who's head over heels crazy in love with you?"

"And you're sure my having Charlie doesn't matter to you?"

"Oh, it matters a lot. I'd love to be the one to teach him to play ball when he's old enough."

"I think Charlie would love having a father."

"But would you love having a husband?"

"Depends on who it is, and since there's only one candidate on my list…"

"Want to go to Ming's tonight and discuss it?"

"I have a better idea. Let's go to your condo and discuss it. Because here's the thing. Now that I'm going to be the mother of two children, I'm dying to have another baby. So I could get a sitter and we could go to your condo and begin to work at making a baby of our own."

"Seriously?"

"You want to be a father, don't you? And I'm assuming it's to be a large family. So one or two more children should round us out nicely."

"Why, I'd love to make a baby with you, Del."

"And I'd love to make a baby with you, Simon." With that, she twined her fingers around his neck and pulled him closer for the kiss that sealed the deal. "I love you," she whispered to him, not caring that they were standing in the middle of the hall where anybody could see them."

"And I love you," he said back, his lips to hers.

"I love the family we have and the one we're going to make together, too," she continued, only this time in a whisper.

"Do we have to wait until tonight to start?"

"Just a minute," she said, then went to the doctors' board and wiped her name off it. "Now, we've got three hours until I have to pick Charlie up from day care."

"And I promised Amy I'd be back at the hospital to have dinner with her. This is our life now," he warned. "You do know that, don't you?"

"I know," she said, taking his hand as they hurried out the clinic door. "And I wouldn't trade it for anything."

As they walked hand in hand down the sidewalk to his condo, which was the closest by a block to the clinic, she looked out over the lake and smiled. Yes, this was her life now. The one she wanted. The one she needed.

The one she loved.

* * * * *

If you enjoyed this story, check out these other great reads from Dianne Drake

TORTURED BY HER TOUCH
A HOME FOR THE HOT-SHOT DOC
A DOCTOR'S CONFESSION
A CHILD TO HEAL THEIR HEARTS

All available now!

MILLS & BOON®

The One Summer Collection!

Join these heroines on a relaxing holiday escape, where a summer fling could turn in to so much more!

Order yours at **www.millsandboon.co.uk/onesummer**

0616_MB523_OSA